Paddington Takes the Air

Paddington Takes the Air

MICHAEL BOND

Illustrated by Peggy Fortnum

A YEARLING BOOK

Published by
Dell Publishing Co., Inc.
1 Dag Hammarskjold Plaza
New York, New York 10017

Yearling ® TM 913705, Dell Publishing Co., Inc.
ISBN: 0-440-47321-7
Reprinted by arrangement with Houghton Mifflin Company
Printed in the United States of America
Fifth Dell Printing—March 1977

CONTENTS

CHAPTER ONE

A Visit to the Dentist

Paddington stared at Mrs. Brown as if he could hardly believe his ears. "You've dropped my tooth down the waste-disposal!" he exclaimed. "I shan't even be able to put it under my pillow now!"

Mrs. Brown peered helplessly into the gaping hole at the bottom of her kitchen sink. "I'm awfully sorry, dear," she replied. "It must have been in the leavings when I cleared up after breakfast. I think you'll have to leave a note explaining what happened."

It was a tradition in the Browns' household that anyone who lost a tooth and left it under their pillow that night would find it replaced by a sixpence the next morning and Paddington looked most upset at being deprived of this experience.

"Perhaps we could try looking under the cover outside," suggested Judy hopefully. "It might still be in the drain."

"I shouldn't think so," said Jonathan. "Those waste-disposals are jolly good. They grind up anything. It even managed that ever-lasting toffee Paddington gave me yesterday."

"It was a super one," he added hastily, as he caught Paddington's eye. "I wish I could make one half as nice. It was a bit big, though. I couldn't quite finish it."

"Well," said Mr. Brown, returning to the vexed question of Paddington's tooth, "at least it didn't jam the machine. We've only had it a fortnight."

But if Mr. Brown was trying to strike a cheerful note he failed miserably, for Paddington gave him a very hard stare indeed.

"I've had my tooth ever since I was born," he said. "And it was my best one. I don't know what Aunt Lucy's going to say when I write and tell her."

And with that parting shot he hurried out of the kitchen and disappeared upstairs in the direction of his room leaving behind a very unhappy group of Browns indeed.

"I don't see how anyone can have a *best* tooth," said Mr. Brown, as he made ready to leave for the office.

"Well," said Mrs. Bird, their housekeeper, "best or not, I must say I don't blame that bear. I don't think I'd be too happy at the thought of one of my teeth going down a waste-disposal—even if it was an accident."

"It would have to be Paddington's," said Judy. "You know how he hates losing anything. Especially when it's something he's cleaned twice a day."

"We shall never hear the last of it," agreed Mrs. Brown. She looked round the kitchen at the remains of the breakfast things. "I do hate Mondays. I don't know why, but there always seems to be more dried egg on the plates than any other day."

The others fell silent. It was one of those mornings at number thirty-two Windsor Gardens. Things had started badly when Paddington announced that he'd found a bone in his boiled egg, but remembering a similar occurrence some years before with a Christmas pudding, the Browns had pooh-poohed the idea at first and it wasn't until a little later on when he'd gone upstairs to do his Monday morning accounts that the trouble had really begun.

A sudden cry of alarm had brought the rest of the family racing to the scene only to find Paddington on his bed with a pencil stuck between a large gap where one of his back teeth should have been.

Immediately the whole house had been in an uproar. The bed was stripped, carpets were turned back, the vacuum cleaner emptied, pockets turned out; Paddington even tried standing on his head in case he'd swallowed the lost half by mistake, but all to no avail . . . it was nowhere to be seen.

It wasn't until Mrs. Bird remembered the episode with the boiled egg that they suddenly put two and two together and went scurrying back downstairs again as fast as their legs would carry them.

But they were too late. Before they were halfway down they heard a loud grinding noise coming from the kitchen and they arrived there just in time to see Mrs. Brown switch the machine off.

The waste-disposal was still a new toy in the household. Everything from used matchsticks to old bones was fed into its ever-open mouth, but never in her wildest moments would Mrs. Brown have dreamed of disposing of one of Paddington's teeth and she was as upset as anyone when she realised what had happened.

"I can't see them taking him on the National Health," she said. "Perhaps he'd better go to the vet."

"Certainly not," said Mrs. Bird decidedly. "He'll have to go as a private patient. I'll ring Mr. Leach straight away."

Although the Browns' housekeeper kept a firm hand on Paddington's "goings on" she was always quick to come to his aid in time of trouble and she bustled out of the room in a very determined manner.

All the same, the others awaited her return with some anxiety, for although Mr. Leach had looked after the family's teeth for more years than they cared to remember, he'd never actually been asked to deal with one of Paddington's before. They weren't at all sure how he would view the matter and their spirits rose when Mrs. Bird reappeared wearing her coat and hat.

"Mr. Leach will see him as soon as we can get there,"

she announced. "He keeps a free period for emergencies."

Mrs. Brown heaved a sigh of relief. "How nice," she said. "It's not as if we've ever registered Paddington with him."

"Who said anything about Paddington?" replied Mrs. Bird innocently. "I simply said we have an emergency in the house." She glanced up at the ceiling as a loud groan came from somewhere overhead. "And if you ask me there's no one who'll deny the truth of that! I'd better order a taxi."

While Mrs. Bird got busy on the phone again the others hurried upstairs to see how Paddington was getting on. They found him sitting on the side of his bed wearing a very woebegone expression on his face indeed. Or rather, the little of his face that could be seen, for most

of it was concealed behind a large bath towel. Every so often a low groan issued from somewhere deep inside the folds, and if the news of his forthcoming visit to the dentist did little to raise his spirits they received a further set-back a few minutes later when he was ushered into the back of a waiting taxi.

"'Aving trouble with yer choppers, mate?" asked the driver catching sight of the towel.

"My *choppers?*" exclaimed Paddington.

"I only 'ope he's not a strong union man," continued the driver as they moved away. "One out—the lot out!"

Mrs. Brown hastily closed the window between the two compartments. "Don't take any notice, dear," she said. "I'm sure you're doing the right thing. Mr. Leach is very good. He's been practising for years."

"Mr. Leach has been *practising?*" repeated Paddington with growing alarm. "I think I'd sooner pay extra and have someone who knows what he's doing."

The Browns exchanged glances. It was sometimes very difficult explaining things to Paddington—especially when he had his mind firmly fixed on something else—and they completed the rest of the journey in silence.

However, if Paddington himself was beginning to have mixed feelings on the subject of his tooth, Mr. Leach had no such problems when they reached his surgery a short while later.

"I'm afraid I shall have to charge extra," he said, as the situation was explained to him. "Bears have forty-two teeth."

"I've only got forty-one," said Paddington. "One of mine's been disposed of."

"That's still nine more than I normally deal with," said Mr. Leach firmly, ushering Paddington into his surgery. "None of my charts cover it for a start. I shall have to get my nurse to draw up a completely new one."

"I do hope we *are* doing the right thing," said Mrs. Brown anxiously, as the door closed behind them. "I feel it's all my fault."

Mrs. Bird gave a snort. "More likely that bear's everlasting toffees," she said grimly. "They're well named. It's almost impossible to get rid of them. It's no wonder he's lost a tooth. He was testing them all day yesterday. I had to throw the saucepan away and there were toffees all over the kitchen floor. I nearly ricked my ankle twice."

Paddington's home-made toffees were a sore subject in the Brown household. It wasn't so much that they had set hard. In fact, had they done so there might have been fewer complaints, but they'd ended up as a pile of large glutinous balls which stuck to everything they came in contact with, and Mrs. Bird spent the next few minutes holding forth on what she would like to do with them.

However, it was noticeable that all the while she was talking the Browns' housekeeper kept her gaze firmly fixed on the door leading to the surgery, rather as if she wished she had X-ray eyes.

But as it happened for once Mrs. Bird's worst fears weren't being realised, for Paddington was beginning to have second thoughts about dentists.

Looking round Mr. Leach's surgery he decided it was all very much nicer than he'd expected. Everything was gleaming white and spotlessly clean, with not a marmalade stain to be seen anywhere. And although it wasn't what Mrs. Bird would have called "over-furnished" the one chair Mr. Leach did possess more than made up for the fact.

Paddington had never come across anything quite like it before. It was like a long couch which rose into the air and took on all kinds of shapes simply at the press of a button. It seemed very good value indeed and Paddington was most impressed.

Above his head there was a nice, warm lamp and just beside his left paw there was a glass of pinkish liquid and a basin, whilst on the other side, next to Mr. Leach, there was a table fixed to an arm on which a number of instruments were laid.

Paddington hastily averted his gaze from these as he settled back in the chair, but he liked anything new and despite his aching tooth he dutifully opened his mouth and eyed Mr. Leach with interest as the latter picked up a small rod-like object and what looked like a mirror on the end of a stick.

Mr. Leach gave several grunts of approval as he peered into Paddington's mouth, tapping the teeth one by one with the end of the rod, and several times he broke into song as he delved deeper and deeper.

"We've got a good one there, bear," he said, standing up at last. "I'm glad you came along."

Paddington sat up looking most relieved. "Thank you very much, Mr. Leach," he exclaimed. "That didn't hurt a bit."

Mr. Leach looked slightly taken aback. "I haven't done anything yet," he said. "That was only an inspection —just to see what's what. We've a long way to go yet. I'm afraid you have a fractured cusp."

"What!" exclaimed Paddington hotly. "My cusp's fractured!" He peered at the rod in Mr. Leach's hand. "It was all right when I came in," he added meaningly. "I think it must have happened when you tapped it."

"A fractured cusp," said Mr. Leach stiffly, as he busied himself with the tray of instruments, "merely means you have a broken tooth." He wagged his finger roguishly. "I have a feeling we've been eating something we shouldn't."

Paddington sank back in his chair and looked at the dentist with renewed interest. "Have you been making toffee too, Mr. Leach?" he exclaimed.

Mr. Leach gave Paddington a strange look. "You have quite a large piece of double tooth missing," he said, slowly and carefully, "and I shall have to make you a new top to replace it."

Looking most upset at this latest piece of news, Paddington reached out a paw for the nearby glass of pink liquid. "I think I'll have my orangeade now, Mr. Leach, if you don't mind," he exclaimed.

"That," said Mr. Leach sternly, "is *not* orangeade. It's not even for drinking. It's put there so that you can swill

your mouth out and get rid of the bits and pieces after
I've finished drilling. If I kept every young bear who
came in here supplied with free drinks I'd soon be out
of business."

He looked distastefully at Paddington's front where
the fur had already become rather soggy from the drips
and then signalled his nurse to tie a plastic bib round
Paddington's neck. "Would we like an injection?" he
asked. "It may hurt otherwise."

"Yes, please," said Paddington promptly. "I'll have
two if you like."

"I think one will be sufficient," replied Mr. Leach,
holding a syringe up to the light. "Now, open your mouth
wide, please," he continued. "And don't forget, this is
going to hurt me more than it hurts you."

Paddington dutifully obeyed Mr. Leach's instructions
and, in fact, apart from a slight prick, it was much less
painful than he had expected.

"Shall I do yours now, Mr. Leach?" he asked.

Mr. Leach gave him a strange look. "Mine?" he
repeated. "*I* don't have an injection."

Paddington gave Mr. Leach an equally strange look
in return. "You said *we* were going to have one," he
persisted. "*And* you said yours would hurt more than
mine."

Mr. Leach stared at Paddington for a moment as if he
could hardly believe his ears and then turned to his nurse.
"I think," he said, breathing heavily, "we'll try putting
a wedge in his mouth. It may make things easier."

"Now," he continued, turning back to Paddington as the nurse handed him a piece of plastic-looking material. "I want you to open your mouth again, say 'ah', and when I've put this in take a good, hard bite."

Paddington opened his mouth and let out a loud "aaaah".

"Good," said Mr. Leach approvingly, as he reached into the opening. "Now, one more 'aah' like that and then a good, hard bite. And whatever happens from now—don't let go."

"Aaaaah," said Paddington.

Mr. Leach's face seemed to change colour suddenly. "Ooooooooh," he cried.

"Oooooooooooh," repeated Paddington, biting harder than ever.

"Owwwwwwwwwwwwwww," shouted Mr. Leach, as he began dancing up and down.

"Owwwwwwwwwwwwwwwwwwww," called Paddington, nearly falling out of the chair in his excitement. "Owwwwwwwwwwww!"

"Ouch!" shrieked Mr. Leach. "Owwwwwwww! Ooooooooooooo! Aaaaaaaaaaa!"

Outside in the waiting-room the Browns looked anxiously at one another. "Poor old Paddington," said Jonathan. "It sounds as if he's going through it."

"I do hope it doesn't take much longer," said Mrs. Brown. "I don't know about Paddington, but I'm not sure if I can stand a lot more."

As it happened Mrs. Brown's prayers were answered

almost before the words were out of her mouth, for at that moment the surgery door burst open and a white-faced nurse appeared in the opening.

"Can you come quickly?" she cried.

Mrs. Brown clutched at her throat. "Paddington!" she cried. "He's not . . ."

"No," said the nurse, "he's not! We haven't even started on *him* yet. It's Mr. Leach we're having trouble with."

Mrs. Bird hurried into the surgery clutching her umbrella. "Whatever's going on?" she demanded.

"Aaaaaaaaaaaah," replied Paddington.

"Oooooooooooh!" shrieked Mr. Leach. "Ooooh! Ouch! Aaaaaaaah!"

"Crikey!" exclaimed Jonathan, as he and Judy dashed towards the chair where Paddington and Mr. Leach appeared to be inextricably locked together.

"You grab Mr. Leach," cried Judy. "I'll pull Paddington."

A moment later Mr. Leach staggered back across the room. "My thumb," he said, slowly and distinctly as he glared at the occupant of the chair, "my thumb—or what's left of it—was caught under your wedge, bear!"

Paddington put on his injured expression. "You said bite hard and not let go whatever happened, Mr. Leach," he explained.

Mrs. Brown gazed anxiously at the dentist as he stood in the middle of the surgery nursing his injury. "Would you like us to come back another day?" she asked doubtfully.

Mr. Leach appeared for a moment to be undergoing some kind of deep internal struggle and then he took a grip of himself. "No," he said at last. "No! When I became a dentist I knew there would be days when things wouldn't always go right." He looked at Paddington and then reached for his drill. "I've had twenty most enjoyable years. I suppose it had to come to an end some time and I'm certainly not letting a bear's cusp get the better of me now!"

It was some time before Paddington emerged again from Mr. Leach's surgery, and although all had remained quiet the Browns were relieved to see him looking none the worse for his experience. Indeed, as he hurried into the waiting-room holding his mouth open for all to see, he looked positively excited.

"Mr. Leach is going to give me a new gold tooth," he announced importantly. "My cusp's so large he doesn't think an ordinary one would stand the strain."

Mr. Leach permitted himself a smile as he hovered in the doorway nursing a bandaged thumb. "I think we're winning at long last," he said. "I'd like to see young Mr. Brown again next week for a final fitting."

"Thank you very much, Mr. Leach," said Paddington gratefully. Bending down he undid his suitcase, withdrew a large paper-bag, and held it out. "Perhaps you'd like to try one of these?"

Mr. Leach hesitated. "I . . . er . . . I don't normally

19

indulge," he said, peering into the bag. "It doesn't set a very good example. But I must say they look tempting. It's very kind of you. I . . . er . . ."

As he placed one of Paddington's ever-lasting toffees into his mouth Mr. Leach's voice trailed away and for the second time that morning his face took on a glazed expression.

"Grrrrrrr," he gurgled, pointing to his mouth. "Glug!"

Paddington peered at him with interest. "I hope you haven't fractured one of *your* cusps now, Mr. Leach," he said anxiously.

Mr. Leach glared at him for a moment and then staggered back into his surgery clutching his jaw. Far from being fractured his cusps gave the impression they were cemented together for all time and the look on his face as he slammed the door boded ill for the next patient on his list that morning.

Paddington looked most upset. "I only thought he would like one to be going on with," he exclaimed.

"Going on with is right," said Mrs. Bird grimly, as a series of muffled exclamations reached their ears. "By the sound of things it'll be going on until this time next week."

She held out her hand. "I know something else that's due to be disposed of just as soon as we get home. We've had quite enough bear's ever-lasting toffee for one day."

Judy squeezed Paddington's paw as they climbed into a taxi to take them home. "Never mind," she whispered.

"There can't be many bears who are able to say they're having a gold tooth made for them."

"I'll tell you something else," said Mrs. Brown. "It'll make you even more valuable than you are at the moment. While you have a gold tooth in your head you'll never be completely without—whatever else happens."

Paddington digested this latest piece of information for a moment or two as he settled back in his seat. So much had happened that morning he felt he'd have a job to remember it all let alone put it down on a postcard when he next wrote to his Aunt Lucy in Peru. But all in all he was beginning to feel rather pleased at the way things had turned out and he felt sure she would be equally delighted by the news.

Mrs. Bird glanced across at him with the suspicion of a twinkle in her eye. "If this morning's events are anything to go by," she said, "it strikes me that a tooth in the sink is worth two under the pillow any day of the week."

Paddington nodded his agreement. "I think," he announced at last, amid sighs of relief, "I'll always have my old teeth disposed of in future."

CHAPTER TWO

A Stitch in Time

Mrs. Bird held a large square of chequered cloth up to the light and examined it with an expert eye. "I must say Paddington's made a first-class job of it," she declared approvingly.

"I've seen worse in some shops," agreed Mrs. Brown. "What is it?"

"I think he said it's a table-cloth," replied Mrs. Bird. "But whatever it is I'm sure it'll come in very handy."

Mrs. Brown glanced up at the ceiling as a steady rhythmic clanking came from somewhere overhead. "At least we can leave him on his own for the day without worrying too much," she said thankfully. "We may as well make the most of it. At the rate he's going that sewing machine won't last much longer."

Mrs. Brown was never very happy about leaving Paddington on his own for too long. Things had a habit of going wrong—especially on days when he was at a loose end—but with Jonathan and Judy back at school after the Easter holiday it couldn't always be avoided. It happened to be one of those days and she was most relieved to know he was occupied.

Paddington's interest in sewing had been something of a nine-day wonder in the Brown household. It all came about when he lost his one and sixpence a week bun money down a drain one morning as he was on his way to the bakers to pick up his standing order.

The coins had slipped through a hole in one of his duffle-coat pockets, and even the combined efforts of several passing dustmen and a roadsweeper had failed to locate them.

Although Mr. Brown took pity on him and replaced the money, Paddington had been upset for several days afterwards. He still felt he was going to be one and sixpence short for the rest of his life and when some men arrived a few days later to swill out the drains he gave them some very hard stares indeed.

It was Mr. Gruber who finally took his mind off the matter. Mr. Gruber kept an antique shop in the nearby Portobello market and over the years he and Paddington had become firm friends. In fact, most mornings they shared some buns and a cup of cocoa for their elevenses.

One morning, shortly after his loss, Paddington arrived at the shop only to find a mysterious cloth-covered object standing on a table just inside the door.

At Mr. Gruber's bidding he lifted the cloth, and then nearly fell over backwards with surprise, for there, lo and behold, was a sewing machine. And even more exciting, on the side there was a label—with *his* name on it!

Mr. Gruber waved Paddington's thanks to one side. "We don't want another day like 'the one we don't talk about' in a hurry, Mr. Brown," he said, referring to "bunless Friday" as they'd come to know it.

"I'm afraid it's rather an old one," he continued, as Paddington examined the machine with interest. "It came in a job lot I bought at a sale many years ago and it's been lying under a chair at the back of my shop ever since. But there's a book of instructions and it may do a turn if you want to go over some of your old seams."

Paddington didn't know what to say. Although Mrs. Bird had unpicked the join on his duffle-coat pocket and inserted a double-strength calico lining to make doubly sure for the future, he didn't want to take any more chances and after thanking Mr. Gruber very much he hurried home with the present safely tucked away in his shopping basket on wheels.

Paddington had often watched Mrs. Bird in action with her machine, and once she'd even let him turn the handle, but never in his wildest dreams had he pictured actually owning one himself.

Threading the needle by paw had been his biggest

problem and the first time it had taken him the best part of a day, but once the cotton was safely through the eye of the needle there was no holding him and soon the steady clickety-clack of the machine had begun to echo round the house.

At first he'd contented himself with joining together some old bits of cloth Mrs. Bird found in her sewing-box, but when these ran out he turned his attention to more ambitious things and really and truly he'd been most useful. A new tea towel for Mrs. Bird; a set of curtains for Judy's doll's house; a bag for Jonathan's cricket bat and a smaller one for Mr. Brown's pipe; now the table-cloth—there seemed no end to his activities.

"Just so long as he doesn't do anything nasty to his

new eiderdown," said Mrs. Bird, as they went upstairs to give Paddington his instructions for lunch. "I don't want to come back and find it turned into a tea cosy."

Although the Browns' housekeeper was as pleased as anyone over Paddington's new-found industry she didn't entirely share Mrs. Brown's optimism about leaving him alone for the day.

Nevertheless, even Mrs. Bird gave a nod of approval as they entered his room and she caught sight of a pile of old handkerchiefs he was busy repairing.

"That reminds me," said Mrs. Brown as they said goodbye, "the laundry man is due this morning. I've put the things by the front door. Mr. Curry might call in later—he's got a pair of trousers he wants altered."

Mrs. Bird gave a snort. "I shouldn't worry too much about that," she said meaningly. "It's only because there's a special offer of sixpence off this week if repairs go with the laundry. If he's so mean he can't send any washing of his own then it's too bad."

There was little love lost between Mrs. Bird and the Browns' next-door neighbour. Mr. Curry had a reputation not only for his meanness but for the way he seized every opportunity to take advantage of others, and the latest example lasted Mrs. Bird as a topic of conversation all the way to the bus stop.

It seemed just a matter of seconds after the front door closed behind them that another loud bang sent Paddington hurrying downstairs only to find Mr. Curry waiting impatiently on the front step.

"Good morning, bear," he said gruffly. "I'd like you to put these with your laundry.

"I want two inches off the waist," he continued, handing over a pair of grey flannel trousers, "no more, and certainly no less. The instructions are all on a sheet of paper in one of the pockets. I lost a lot of weight when I was in hospital last year and I've never put it on again. All my clothes are the same."

"Oh dear, Mr. Curry," said Paddington, "I'm sorry to hear that."

In saying he was sorry to hear about Mr. Curry's loss of weight Paddington was speaking the truth, for ever since the unfortunate incident on the golf course when he'd stepped on a marmalade sandwich and ended up in hospital the Browns' neighbour had let no opportunity of mentioning the matter go by.

But to Paddington's relief for once Mr. Curry seemed to have his mind on other things. "I want you to make sure they go in your name," he said. "It's most important. They're doing waistbands for nine and six this week and it's the last day of the offer."

A thoughtful expression came over Paddington's face as he took the trousers from Mr. Curry. "I know someone who would do it for one and sixpence," he said hopefully. "*And* give it back to you to-day!"

"*One and sixpence?*" repeated Mr. Curry. "It seems remarkably cheap. Are you sure they'll do them in a day?"

Paddington nodded. "It isn't a *they*, Mr. Curry," he confided. "It's a *he*."

"Is this person completely reliable, bear?" asked Mr. Curry suspiciously. "I can hardly believe it."

"Oh, yes," said Paddington confidently. "I've known him all my life. He lost his bun money down a drain the other day and now he's trying to make up for it."

Fortunately Paddington's last words were lost on Mr. Curry, who seemed to be busy with his own thoughts. He hesitated for a moment and then came to a decision. "Wait there, bear," he said, turning to go. "This is too good an opportunity to miss."

The Browns' neighbour was gone for several minutes and while he was away the man arrived to collect the weekly wash. Paddington hesitated over the trousers. Although the idea of doing them himself had seemed a very good one at the time, now that he'd taken a closer look he was beginning to have second thoughts on the matter, and he was about to chase after the van when he caught sight of Mr. Curry glaring at him through his bedroom window and hurriedly changed his mind again.

A few moments later the Browns' neighbour emerged from his front door and headed back towards number thirty-two. To Paddington's surprise he was wearing a dressing-gown and carrying a large brown paper parcel in his arms.

"I've decided to go the whole hog, bear," he announced,

as he came up the path. "If this person's as good as you say he is it'll be well worth while."

Paddington's face grew longer and longer as Mr. Curry unwrapped his parcel and revealed not one pair of trousers, but a great pile. In fact, outside of a shop, Paddington couldn't remember ever having seen quite so many pairs of trousers before.

"I'm having the whole lot done," explained Mr. Curry. "Including," he added ominously, "the ones from my best suit."

"You wouldn't like to keep a pair in case of an emergency would you, Mr. Curry?" asked Paddington anxiously.

"An *emergency?*" barked Mr. Curry, catching sight of the look on Paddington's face. "I don't like the sound of that, bear! Are you sure this person will do a good job? If not I'd rather send them with your laundry."

"I'm afraid it's too late now, Mr. Curry," said Paddington unhappily. "It's gone!"

Mr. Curry looked at Paddington sternly. "In that case," he warned, "I shall hold you personally responsible for the safety of my trousers from now on. *And* I shall look forward to their prompt return. I can't go out until they come back, so woe betide you if anything goes wrong.

"I may give you sixpence for going," he added, as Paddington held out his paw hopefully. "It all depends. But I'm certainly not paying the full amount until I see some results."

With that the Browns' neighbour turned on his heels and disappeared in the direction of his house leaving Paddington with a very woebegone expression on his face indeed. For some reason which he could never quite fathom, things always got out of hand when Mr. Curry was around and he was apt to find himself agreeing to do things before he knew what they actually were.

Heaving a deep sigh Paddington gathered up Mr. Curry's parcel and made his way back upstairs in order to consult the instruction book.

Up to now he'd concentrated on the mechanical side of the booklet, which explained the workings of the various parts, but towards the back there were several chapters devoted to what one could do with the needle once it was threaded, and it was to this section that he turned when he'd settled down.

But in the event it proved rather disappointing. As far as he could make out, when the machine was first made very few people seemed to wear trousers, or if they did they were so well made they were seldom in need of repair. Most of the illustrations dealt with some very odd situations indeed. There was a picture of a lady who'd caught her dress on a penny-farthing cycle and another, called DRAMA IN THE DESERT, which showed a man with a large moustache and shorts repairing what was left of his tent after a camel had trodden on it. But any hints and tips to do with trousers as such were conspicuous only by their absence.

Although Paddington was very keen on instruction

books he'd noticed in the past they had a habit of dealing with every kind of situation except the one he most wanted, and the present one was no exception.

According to the closing paragraph anyone who owned a SEW-RITE sewing machine had unlimited horizons, but Paddington could see only two good things on his particular horizon; the Browns were out and unlikely to return for some while, and Mr. Curry was in and unlikely in his present trouserless state to venture out.

However, Paddington wasn't the sort of bear to let things get the better of him if he could possibly help it, and picking up a pair of scissors he poked hopefully at one of Mr. Curry's seams.

To his surprise his efforts were rewarded much sooner than he expected, for without any warning at all the

waistband suddenly parted in the middle. In fact, it was even more successful than he'd intended, for when he pulled at the loose thread there was a rending sound and it travelled right down to the turn-ups at the bottom.

Paddington wasn't quite sure whether it was the direct result of pulling that thread or whether he'd pulled another one by mistake, but when he picked the trousers up to examine them more closely one of the legs fell off.

After drawing his bedroom curtains to be on the safe side Paddington held the remaining leg up to his bedside light and peered at it uneasily. Now that matters had finally come to a head he rather wished he'd sorted through the pile and picked on something other than the trousers from Mr. Curry's best navy-blue pin-stripe suit to practise on.

On the other hand, when he looked at some of his efforts a little later on he began to wonder if perhaps his first choice hadn't been the best one after all. At least the two halves had come apart cleanly, which was more than could be said for some of the older pairs of trousers.

But it was when he tried sewing some of the halves together again that his troubles really started. It was much more difficult than he had expected. In the past most of the material he'd used had been thin and easy to work, whereas Mr. Curry's trousers seemed unusually thick. There were so many folds in his waistbands he soon lost count of them, and the handle of the machine became very hard to turn. In desperation Paddington tried jamming it in one of his dressing-table drawers and turning the machine itself, but the only result of that was an ominous "ping" as the needle snapped.

It was all most disappointing. After working away as hard as he could, with barely a pause for a marmalade sandwich at lunch, Paddington had to admit that the results fell somewhat short of even his own expectations, and he shuddered to think how far short they were of Mr. Curry's.

As far as he could see all he could offer the Browns' neighbour was a choice between a pair of trousers with twelve-inch hips and pockets on the outside, one with a large gap in the back, a pair of grey flannel shorts with one leg longer than the other, some trousers with different coloured legs, or a kind of do-it-yourself selection from the pieces that were left over.

Whichever Mr. Curry chose Paddington couldn't picture him being exactly overjoyed let alone paying one and sixpence a time.

He looked at the pile of material mournfully. For a wild moment he toyed with the idea of disguising his voice and ringing the Browns' neighbour to try and explain matters to him, but then he remembered Mr. Curry wasn't on the phone anyway.

All the same, the thought triggered off another idea in Paddington's mind, and a moment later, after consulting his instruction book again, he hurried downstairs.

In the back of the SEW-RITE booklet was a note headed WHAT TO DO IF ALL ELSE FAILS! and this was followed by an address to write to in case of an emergency.

Paddington hoped very much that they'd had enough emergencies over the years to keep their service going *and* to have a telephone installed into the bargain, though he doubted very much if they could ever have had one quite as bad as his present one.

The man from the SEW-RITE emergency service stared round Paddington's room in amazement. "You're in a bit of a mess and no mistake," he said sympathetically. "What on earth's been going on?"

"I'm afraid I've been having trouble with Mr. Curry's seams," said Paddington. "I've got rather a lot of his legs left over."

"I can see that," said the man, picking up a handful. "This sort of thing isn't really our pigeon," he continued

34

doubtfully, "but I suppose I might be able to pull a few strings for you."

"I've tried pulling some threads," said Paddington, "but it only seemed to make things worse."

The man gave Paddington an odd look and then, glancing round the room again, he gave a sudden start. "Is that yours?" he asked, pointing to the machine on the floor.

"Well, yes," began Paddington. "Mr. Gruber gave it to me. I'm afraid it's rather an old one so you may not like it very much."

"Not like it?" cried the man, dashing to the door. "*Not like it?* Jim!" he shouted. "Jim! There's a young bear up here with one of our Mark One's!"

Paddington grew more and more mystified as a pounding of feet on the stairs heralded the approach of a second man. He wasn't at all sure what was going on but he was thankful to see something happening at long last. It had taken him several telephone calls and some long conversations to get the men from SEW-RITE to come in the first place. Even then he hadn't been at all hopeful about the results, but as he listened to their comments his eyes grew rounder and rounder.

"Just you wait till our Mr. Bridges hears about this," exclaimed the first man, as they made to leave. "He'll go berserk. You'll never hear the like again."

"I expect I shall," said Paddington unhappily. "You wait until Mr. Curry hears about his trousers!"

Although the long-term prospects had begun to look

much better than he'd dared expect Paddington didn't view the immediate future at all hopefully and as things turned out his forecast proved all too correct. The roar of rage which issued from Mr. Curry's house a short while later when the men from SEW-RITE broke the news about his trousers followed him all the way down Windsor Gardens, lasting almost as far as the Portobello Road, and he was very thankful indeed to reach the safety of Mr. Gruber's shop.

While Paddington sat on the horsehair sofa mopping his brow Mr. Gruber hastily made some cocoa and a few minutes later they adjourned to their usual deck-chairs on the pavement outside.

Once there, Mr. Gruber settled back and listened patiently while Paddington did his best to explain all that had taken place that day.

It was a long story and at the finish Mr. Gruber looked as surprised at the outcome as Paddington had done.

"What a bit of luck that old sewing machine I gave you turned out to be so valuable," he said. "I would never have guessed it. It only goes to show that even in this business there's always something to learn."

"The man from SEW-RITE said it's one of their Mark One's, Mr. Gruber," replied Paddington impressively. "He told me it must have been one of the first they ever made. They've been trying to find one like it for years to put in their museum so it's probably worth a lot of money."

"It's a good job they offered to repair Mr. Curry's

trousers free of charge," chuckled Mr. Gruber, pouring out a second cup of cocoa by way of celebration. "We should never have heard the last of it otherwise. It seems to me you struck a very good bargain, Mr. Brown."

"Just think," he mused, "if you hadn't accidentally dropped your bun money down a drain all this might never have happened. Big things sometimes have very small beginnings indeed."

Paddington nodded his agreement behind the cocoa steam and then hesitated as he felt in his duffle-coat pocket.

Mr. Gruber read his thoughts. "I don't think it would be quite the same if you deliberately put some money down a drain, Mr. Brown," he said tactfully. "After all, I know lightning seldom strikes twice in the same place, but fate plays funny tricks sometimes."

Paddington considered the matter for a moment. All in all he decided Mr. Gruber was quite right and it wasn't worth taking any unnecessary risks. "I don't think I should like to see even Mr. Curry's trousers struck by lightning," he announced. "Especially while they're still at the menders!"

CHAPTER THREE

Riding High

Paddington reined in his horse and stared at the judge's rostrum as if he could hardly believe his ears.

"I've got four hundred and fifty-two faults?" he exclaimed hotly. "But I've only been round once!"

"There are twelve fences," said Gay Cheeseman, measuring his words with care, "and you went straight through all of them—that's forty-eight for a start. Plus another four for going back over the last one.

"*And,*" he added, bringing the subject firmly to a close as he glared down at the battered remains of what had once been a hat, "your horse trampled all over my best bowler—the one I intended wearing at the presentation this afternoon—that's another four hundred!"

Mr. Cheeseman wasn't in the best of moods. In fact, the look on his face as he made an entry alongside Paddington's signature on the clip-board he was carrying went ill with his name. Far from being "gay" he gave the distinct impression that he wished he'd never heard of St. Christopher's School and its mistresses and parents in general, not to mention Paddington in particular.

The occasion was the end of term celebration at Judy's school and instead of the usual speech-making Miss Grimshaw, the head-mistress, had decided to hold a gymkhana in aid of a new swimming-pool.

There were a number of events on the programme, and the two main items at the beginning and end were open to all and sundry—including the parents, relations and friends of the pupils.

The competitors were given "sponsor sheets" and each had to collect as many signatures as possible from people who were prepared to pay a small sum for every successful jump.

The Browns arrived quite early in the day and Paddington—who had decided to enter for both the events—had been kept very busy hurrying round the grounds collecting names for his sheet.

He was already a familiar figure at Judy's school and almost the entire upper and lower fourth, fifth and sixth forms had persuaded their nearest and dearest to sponsor him at anything between sixpence and five shillings a jump. In view of the number of signatures Paddington had managed to collect, the swimming-pool fund stood to benefit by a tidy amount.

Gay Cheeseman, the famous Olympic rider, had very kindly agreed to judge the contests and act as commentator, and with the sun shining down from a cloudless

sky, the sound of horses' hooves pounding the turf, the murmur of the large crowd which had gathered round the sports field, and the creaking of innumerable picnic baskets, it promised to be a memorable occasion.

The roar of excitement as Paddington mounted his horse was equalled only by the groan of disappointment which went up as he disappeared from view over the other side. And when he eventually reappeared facing the wrong way an ominous silence fell over the field; a silence broken only by the crash of falling fences and a cry of rage from Mr. Cheeseman as he watched his best hat being ground to pulp.

Paddington was more upset than anyone, for although

he'd never actually been on a horse before, let alone a jumping one, Mr. Gruber had lent him several very good books on the subject and he'd spent the last few evenings sitting astride a pouffe in the Browns' sitting-room practising with a home-made whip and some stirrups made from a pair of Jonathan's old hand-cuffs.

It was all most disappointing. In fact, he rather wished now he'd chosen something else to practise on. To start with, the horse was very much taller and harder than he'd expected—more iron and steel than flesh and blood—and whereas by gripping the pouffe between his knees he'd been able to hop around the house at quite a speed it was nothing compared with Black Beauty once she got going. That apart—aside from when he'd unexpectedly bumped into Mrs. Bird in the hall—he'd never attempted any kind of jumps on the pouffe, and no matter what he shouted to Black Beauty she seemed to have it firmly fixed in her mind that the shortest distance between two points was a straight line, regardless of what happened to be in the way.

According to Mr. Gruber's book one of the first requirements in horse-riding was complete confidence between rider and mount and Paddington would have been the first to admit that as far as he was concerned he was a non-starter in this respect. He completed the round clinging helplessly to Black Beauty's tail with his eyes tightly closed, and the trail of damage they left behind made the hockey pitch at St. Christopher's resemble the fields of Belgium immediately after the battle of Waterloo.

"Never mind, Paddington," said Judy, grabbing hold of the reins. "We all thought you did jolly well."

"Especially as it was your first time out," she added, amid a chorus of sympathetic agreement from the other girls. "Not many people would have dared to try."

"Th . . . th . . . thank you v . . . v v . . . very m . . . m . . . much," stuttered Paddington. He was still feeling as if he'd been for a ride on a particularly powerful pneumatic drill and he gave Mr. Cheeseman a very hard stare indeed as he was helped down to the ground.

"It's a shame really," said Mrs. Brown, as they watched his progress back to the horse enclosure. "It would have made such a nice start to the day if he'd had a clear round."

"Perhaps he'll do better in the 'Chase me Charley'," said Jonathan hopefully. "He's down for that as well at the end."

"Four hundred and fifty-two faults indeed!" snorted Mrs. Bird, as the commentator's voice boomed through the loudspeakers.

"It's a good job *he* didn't tread on *Paddington's* hat. He'd have lost a good deal more than that!"

Giving a final glare in the direction of the judge's rostrum the Browns' housekeeper began busying herself with the picnic basket in a way which boded ill for Mr. Cheeseman's chances of a snack if he found he'd left his own sandwiches at home.

"That's a good idea," said Jonathan enthusiastically. "I'm so hungry I could eat a horse."

"Pity you didn't eat Paddington's," said Mr. Brown gloomily. "Especially after that last round."

"Ssh, Henry," whispered Mrs. Brown. "Here he comes. We don't want to upset him any more."

Mr. Brown hastily turned his attention to the important matter of lunch and as the fences were put back and the next event got under way he began setting up a table and chair in the shade of a nearby oak tree. Mr. Brown didn't believe in doing things by halves, especially where picnics were concerned, and he shared the French habit of turning such affairs into a full-scale family occasion.

Mrs. Bird had packed an enormous hamper of jars and plastic containers brimful with sliced tomatoes, cucumber, beetroot, ham, beef, liver-sausage, and seemingly endless supplies of mixed salads. What with these and strawberries and cream to follow, not to mention two sorts of ice-cream, lemonade, tea, coffee, various cakes and sweetmeats, and a jar of Paddington's favourite marmalade into the bargain, the table was soon groaning under the weight.

Even Mr. Brown, who wasn't normally too keen on equestrian events, had to admit that he couldn't think of a more pleasant way of spending a summer afternoon. And as event followed event and the contents of the hamper grew less and less, the bad start to the day was soon forgotten.

Paddington himself had worked up quite an appetite,

though for once he seemed more interested in Mr. Gruber's book on riding, which he'd brought with him in case of an emergency, rather than in the actual food itself. Several times he dipped his paw into the bowl of salad-dressing in mistake for the marmalade as he studied

a particularly interesting chapter on jumping which he hadn't read before, and apart from suddenly rearing up into the air once or twice as he went through the motions, he remained remarkably quiet.

It wasn't until nearly the end of the meal when he absent-mindedly reached into the basket and helped himself to one of Mrs. Bird's meringues that he showed any signs of life at all.

"Aren't they delicious?" said Mrs. Brown. "I don't think I've ever tasted better."

"Don't you like them, Paddington?" asked Mrs. Bird, looking most concerned at the expression on his face.

"Er . . . yes, Mrs. Bird," said Paddington politely. "They're . . . er . . . they're very unusual. I think I'll put some marmalade on to take the taste . . . to er . . ."

Paddington's voice trailed away. Although not wishing to say so he didn't think much of Mrs. Bird's meringue at all and he was glad it was particularly small and dainty. It was really most unusual, for Mrs. Bird was an extremely good cook and her cakes normally melted in the mouth, whereas the present one not only showed no signs of melting but was positively stringy.

And it wasn't just the texture. Paddington couldn't make up his mind if it was because he'd followed the ice-cream with another helping of Russian salad or whether Mr. Brown had accidentally spilled some paraffin over it when he'd filled the picnic stove, but whatever the reason Mrs. Bird's meringue was very odd indeed and not even a liberal splodge of marmalade entirely took the taste away.

However, Paddington was a polite bear and he had no wish to offend anyone, least of all Mrs. Bird, so he manfully carried on. Fortunately he was saved any further embarrassment by Gay Cheeseman announcing that the final event on the programme was about to take place and asking the competitors to come forward.

Hastily cramming the remains of the meringue into

his mouth, Paddington gathered up his book and sponsor
sheet and hurried off in the direction of the saddling
enclosure closely followed by Judy and several of her
friends.

"I know one thing," said Mr. Brown, as he disappeared from view into the crowd, "if he manages to
get over *one* fence the swimming-pool fund won't do
too badly. He's got enough signatures now to float a
battleship."

For various reasons Paddington's sponsor sheet had
grown considerably during the course of the afternoon.
Apart from a number of people who'd added their names
a second time to show they hadn't lost faith, there was a
considerable new element who had signed for quite a
different reason—sensing that in backing Paddington
they could show willing without too great an expense,
and his sheet was now jam-packed with signatures.

"It would serve some of them right if he did do well,"
said Mrs. Bird darkly. "It might teach them a lesson."

Mrs. Bird looked as if she'd been about to add a great
deal more but at that moment a burst of applause heralded
the first of the long line of competitors.

The "Chase me Charley" event was one in which all
the contestants formed up in a circle, their horses nose-
to-tail, and took it in turns to jump a single pole. Only
one fault was allowed and each time a round had been
completed those with faults dropped out and the pole
was raised another inch until the final winner emerged.

Practically everyone who could ride was taking part

and the circle of horses stretched right round the field so that it was some time before Paddington came into view on Black Beauty.

There was a nasty moment when he came past the Browns and tried to raise his hat, which he'd insisted on wearing on top of his compulsory riding one, but he soon righted himself and disappeared from view again, holding the reins with one paw and anxiously consulting Mr. Gruber's book which he still held in the other.

"Oh dear," said Mrs. Brown nervously, "I do hope he takes care. I didn't like to say so in his presence but it must be terribly difficult with short legs. No wonder his paws keep coming out of the stirrups."

"I shouldn't worry," said Mrs. Bird. "There's one thing about bears—they always fall on their feet no matter what happens."

Mrs. Bird did her best to sound cheerful but she looked as worried as anyone as they waited for Paddington to make his first jump. Judy arrived back just in the nick of time and in the excitement only Mrs. Bird's sharp eyes noticed that she, too, was now wearing a very odd expression on her face. An expression, moreover, which was almost identical to the one Paddington had worn a little earlier when he'd had trouble with his meringue. But before she had time to look into the matter her attention was drawn back to the field as a great roar went up from the crowd.

The Browns watched in amazement as Paddington and Black Beauty literally sailed over the pole. One moment they'd been trotting gently towards it, then Paddington appeared to lean forward and whisper something in the horse's ear. The very next instant horse and rider leapt into the air and cleared the hurdle with several feet to spare. Admittedly the pole was at its lowest mark but even so the performance drew a gasp of astonishment from the onlookers.

"Bravo!" cried someone near the Browns. "That bear's done it at last. And not even a sign of a refusal!"

"Heavens above!" exclaimed Mr. Brown, twirling his moustache with excitement, "if he carries on like that he'll be up among the leaders in no time. Did you see it? He went higher than anyone!"

Jonathan listened to his sister as she whispered in his ear. "*If* he does it again," he said gloomily.

"Well, even if he doesn't he's certainly not bottom this time," said Mrs. Brown thankfully, as a following rider brought the pole down with a clatter.

And as it happened Jonathan's worst fears went unrealised, for seeming miracle began to follow miracle as Paddington and Black Beauty made one effortless clear round after another and one by one the other competitors began to drop out.

Each time they drew near to the jump Paddington leaned over and appeared to whisper something in Black Beauty's ear and each time it had a magical effect as she bounded into action and with a whinny which echoed round the cloisters, cleared the hurdle with feet to spare.

Paddington was so excited he discarded Mr. Gruber's

book in order to raise his hat in acknowledgment of the cheers, and even those who'd signed his sheet rather late in the day, although they'd worn long faces at first, began applauding with the rest.

And when it came to the final round, with Paddington pitted against Diana Ridgeway, the head girl, the excitement was intense. Even with loyalties so divided the cheer which rang out as Paddington emerged the victor practically shook the school to its foundations, and Diana Ridgeway herself set the seal on the occasion by dismounting and running over to offer her congratulations.

Gay Cheeseman so far forgot the unpleasantness earlier in the day that phrases like "superb horsemanship", "splendid display", and "supreme example of rider and mount being as one", floated round the grounds with scarcely a pause for breath.

For some reason or other Diana Ridgeway appeared to have second thoughts as Paddington leaned down to speak to her, but with an obvious effort she overcame them and in the general excitement the moment passed practically unnoticed.

"What an incredible business!" exclaimed Mr. Brown, mopping his brow as he settled down again. "I wonder what on earth Paddington kept whispering to Black Beauty? It must have been something pretty good to make her want to jump like that."

Jonathan and Judy exchanged glances, then Judy took a deep breath. "I'm not sure he *whispered* anything," she began, only to break off again as she suddenly caught sight of Paddington and the headmistress about to converge a short distance away.

"Crikey! That's torn it," said Jonathan, as Miss Grimshaw began pumping Paddington's paw up and down.

"Stout effort!" she cried. "Allow me to shake you by the paw. You've given our swimming-pool a tremendous fillip."

Paddington began to look more and more surprised as he listened to the headmistress. He had no idea they'd dug the hole even let alone filled it up. "I hope I haven't filled it too full, Miss Grimshaw," he exclaimed politely.

Miss Grimshaw's smile seemed to become strangely

fixed, then she paused and gave a sniff. "I really must get Birchwood to look at the drains," she said, eyeing Paddington even more doubtfully. "I ... er ... I hope we shall meet again at the presentation."

"Crumbs!" said Judy, as the headmistress hurried on her way. "The presentation! We'd better do something before then."

Dashing over to Paddington she grabbed hold of his paw and then turned to her brother. "Come on, Jonathan," she called. "We'll take him to see matron. She's just over there in the First Aid tent. She may be able to give him something."

"Matron?" echoed Mrs. Brown, as Judy began whispering in Paddington's ear. "What on earth are they on about?"

"It's all right, Mrs. Brown," cried Paddington. "It's nothing serious. I'm afraid I'm having trouble with one of Mrs. Bird's meringues."

"Trouble with one of my *meringues*?" Mrs. Bird began to look thoughtful as Judy and Jonathan whisked Paddington away. "How many did the children have?" she asked, rummaging in the picnic basket.

"Three each, I think," replied Mrs. Brown. "I remember them talking about it. Jonathan wanted another but there weren't any left. I had two—the same as you." She turned to her husband. "How many did you have, Henry?"

"Er . . . four," said Mr. Brown. "They were a bit moreish."

"That makes fourteen altogether," said Mrs. Bird, as she began emptying the contents of the picnic basket. "And that's all I made," she added ominously. "So whatever that bear ate it certainly wasn't a meringue!"

Mr. Brown wound down the window of his car to its fullest extent and then glanced across at Paddington. "How anyone could mistake a head of garlic for a meringue I just don't know," he said.

"Especially one of Mrs. Bird's," said Judy. "Matron couldn't believe her ears."

"Or her nose!" added Jonathan.

Paddington looked at them sheepishly. "I'm afraid I was busy reading about my cavalletti's," he explained. "That's to do with jumping. I didn't notice I'd made a mistake until it was too late."

"But a whole head," said Mrs. Brown from behind her handkerchief. "I mean . . . a clove would have been bad enough, but a *whole head*!"

"No wonder Black Beauty was jumping so well," said Judy. "Every time you leaned over her she must have got the full force."

"It's a wonder she didn't go into orbit," agreed Jonathan.

The Browns were making all possible speed in the direction of Windsor Gardens, but even with all the windows open there was a decided "air" about the car.

Paddington had been standing on the front seat with his head poking out of the sunshine roof for most of the way, and every time they stopped they got some very funny looks indeed from any passers-by who happened to be down wind.

"I'll say one thing," remarked Mr. Brown, as they drew to a halt alongside a policeman who hastily waved them on again, "it soon clears the traffic. I don't think we've ever made better time."

"Perhaps I could eat some garlic when we go out again, Mr. Brown?" said Paddington, anxious to make amends.

Mr. Brown gave a shudder. "No, thank you," he said. "Once is quite enough."

"Anyway," broke in Judy, "all's well that ends well. There were over two hundred signatures on Paddington's sheet and Miss Grimshaw reckons it must be worth at least as many pounds to the fund."

"Mr. Cheeseman said he'd never seen anything like it before," said Jonathan.

"Nor will he again if I have anything to do with it," said Mrs. Bird grimly. "That's the last time I make any meringues."

In the chorus of dismay which greeted this last remark Paddington's voice was loudest of all.

"Perhaps you could make them extra large, Mrs. Bird," he said hopefully. "Then they won't get mistaken."

The Browns' housekeeper remained silent for a moment. All in all, despite everything, it had been a most enjoyable day and she was the last person to want to spoil it. "Perhaps you're right," she said, relenting at last. "But you must promise not to go riding on the pouffe when we get home."

Paddington didn't take long to make up his mind. Although he was much too polite to say so the events of the day were beginning to catch up on him and sitting down, even on the softest of pouffes, was the last thing he had in mind.

"I think," he announced, amid general laughter as he clambered up on the seat again. "I shall go to sleep standing up tonight!"

CHAPTER FOUR

Paddington Strikes a Bargain

Next morning Mr. Gruber had a good laugh when he heard about Paddington's exploits at the gymkhana.

"It's strange that you should have spent your day riding a horse, Mr. Brown," he said. "I spent most of mine tinkering with what's known as a *horseless* carriage."

Leading the way across the patio at the back of his shop towards a nearby mews stable which he normally reserved for emergency supplies of antiques during the busy tourist season, Mr. Gruber threw open the wide double doors and then stood back and waited patiently while Paddington accustomed his eyes to the gloom.

"It's what's known as an "old crock", Mr. Brown," he said impressively.

"Is it really?" said Paddington politely.

Although he didn't like to say so, the object of Mr. Gruber's fond gaze seemed very aptly named. From the little he could make out it looked for all the world like a very old boiler on wheels to which an enormously tall push-chair had been added as a kind of after-thought.

Mr. Gruber chuckled as he caught sight of the expression on Paddington's face. "I thought it might puzzle you, Mr. Brown," he said. "I don't suppose you've ever seen anything quite like it before. It's a very early steam-driven motor car. One of the first ever made in fact. I came across it quite by chance the other week and I've been keeping it as a surprise."

Paddington's eyes grew wider and wider as Mr. Gruber went on to explain about early motor cars and how valuable some of them had become over the years, and he listened with growing interest to the story of the first "horseless carriages". Knowing how crowded the

57

present-day London streets were it was difficult to picture the scene as Mr. Gruber described it, and he was most surprised to learn that cars used to have someone walking in front of them carrying a red flag.

Mr. Gruber, who was obviously very proud of his stroke of good fortune, turned to his new machine and gave it a fond pat. "I doubt if there's another one quite like it in the whole of England, Mr. Brown," he said impressively. "I'm afraid it's in a bit of a state at the moment because it's spent most of its life in a hay barn, but if you can spare the time I did wonder if we could do it up between us."

For once in his life Paddington was at a loss for words. Although Mr. Brown sometimes let him clean the family car, and on very rare occasions gave him a spanner to hold, he'd never before been asked to actually help in doing one up. "Oooh, yes please, Mr. Gruber!" he exclaimed at last.

But Mr. Gruber had kept his most exciting piece of news until last.

"There's a big Festival taking place in the Portobello Road in September," he continued, closing the stable door as he led the way back to his shop. "It's called INTERNATIONAL WEEK and it's for the benefit of all the overseas visitors. On the last day there's even going to be a Fair and a Grand Parade through the market."

As they settled down again Mr. Gruber looked at Paddington thoughtfully over the top of his glasses. "If we manage to get the car finished in time," he said casually, "I did wonder if we could enter it."

Paddington stared at his friend in amazement. Over the years Mr. Gruber had sprung a good many surprises but this one surpassed all his previous efforts, and shortly afterwards, bidding him goodbye, he hurried back in the direction of Windsor Gardens in order to tell the others.

Paddington's news met with a mixed reception in the Brown household. Jonathan and Judy were most impressed at the thought of knowing anyone who actually owned an "old crock", and when Paddington announced that Mr. Gruber had promised to reserve them two seats in the car if it was ready in time for the Grand Parade their excitement knew no bounds. But Mrs. Bird, with thoughts of oily paws on her best towels, looked less enthusiastic about the whole idea.

Nevertheless, it was noticeable during the next few weeks that as Paddington began to arrive home with descriptions of the work in progress even the Browns' housekeeper began to take an interest in the matter, and on several occasions she was seen hovering at the end of the mews when she was out doing the morning shopping.

What with dismantling the engine and rebuilding it, rubbing down the coachwork ready for repainting and varnishing, polishing the boiler and refurnishing the leather seats, time flew by at an alarming rate and the gap between Mr. Gruber's first announcement and the day of the actual Parade rapidly narrowed.

Towards the end practically everyone became involved

in one way or another, and most nights found Paddington spreading newspapers on his bedroom floor so that he could catch up on polishing some of the many smaller bits and pieces before he went to bed.

During all this time a great change came over the market itself. Shop windows that had remained untouched for years suddenly took on a new lease of life, and some of the more recent establishments dealing in old army uniforms and other colourful relics of a bygone

era began to look very gay indeed. Flags and bunting blossomed from bedroom windows and coloured lights appeared across the narrow street, so that altogether it was not unlike the transformation scene in a Christmas pantomime.

One evening Paddington arrived home later than usual and his news that Mr. Gruber's "old crock" was ready at long last gave rise to great excitement in the Brown household.

"I know one thing," said Mrs. Bird, when the clamour had died down, "if you're going to be in the Grand Parade tomorrow you'd better have a good bath and get rid of all that oil and grease. You'll never win a prize otherwise."

"You can use some of Mr. Brown's bubble-mixture as a treat if you like," said Mrs. Brown, ignoring the dark glances from her husband.

Paddington, who wasn't normally too keen on baths, brightened considerably at the news.

He'd had his eye on Mr. Brown's jar of bubble-mixture for some time. According to the label on the side even a single capful of the secret ingredients produced un-dreamed of magical results, and although Mr. Brown himself had managed to get through almost half the bottle with little outward sign of any change Paddington felt sure it was worth a go, particularly if it helped Mr. Gruber win a prize.

Carefully making sure no one was around he added several extra helpings to his bath water that night in order to make sure the effect lasted until the following day.

When he arrived down for breakfast next morning everyone had to admit they'd never seen him looking quite so silky before.

"It almost seems a pity to cover it up," said Mrs. Brown as she helped him on with his duffle-coat. "If it was a shiny fur competition you'd be bound to win first prize."

The Browns weren't the only ones to be impressed by Paddington's appearance and as Mr. Gruber's "old crock" steamed into position a little later on, its polished paint and brasswork gleaming in the morning sun, quite a few of the early morning spectators gave him a special round of applause.

A large area of waste ground near the Portobello Road had been set aside for the festivities and already it was a scene of great activity. The centre of the area had been roped off for some games that were to start the proceedings, while almost the whole of one side was occupied by a travelling Fair, and as the various floats and vehicles arrived to take up their position for the Grand Parade the picture grew gayer with every passing moment.

Mr. Gruber gave a tactful cough as they dismounted. "Why don't you have a look round, Mr. Brown?" he said. "I have to take one of the front wheels off to make

some last minute adjustments, but I shall be quite all right on my own."

Paddington hesitated for a moment, torn between helping his friend and investigating some of the other exciting things that were going on around him, but Mr. Gruber clinched the matter by helping him off with his coat. "I should make the most of it, Mr. Brown," he said. "You're only young once."

Paddington needed no second bidding and a few moments later he joined the crowds already thronging the area.

Hoping to find out about Mr. Gruber's chances of winning a prize he tried visiting a Fortune-teller first. But the lady inside the tent seemed to spend most of the time blowing her nose violently into a large coloured handkerchief and when he inquired about his own future all she forecast was that he would probably get a nasty cold, so he decided to turn his attention to the important matter of the games which were about to get under way. A number of the local shops had presented prizes for the various events and Paddington consulted his programme with interest. Although he couldn't quite picture himself shining in the high jump—or even the long one come to that—there were several other items which interested him, including one called TOSSING THE CABER. The prize for this particular event was a free supply of buns for a month at his local bakers.

It seemed very good value indeed and although Paddington wasn't at all sure what a caber was he felt quite certain he could toss one given half a chance.

Going up to a man wearing a kilt he tapped him importantly on the shoulder. "Excuse me," he said politely, "I'd like to toss your caber if I may."

The man in charge looked Paddington up and down. "I hope ye ken what you're takin' on," he said dolefully. "It's no for the like o' young Sassenach bears."

"Sassenach bears?" repeated Paddington, giving the man a hard stare, "I'm not a Sassenach bear. I'm from Darkest Peru. Besides, Mrs. Bird often lets me have a go with her pancakes."

"*Pancakes?*" The man stared at Paddington as if he could hardly believe his ears. "Och, weel," he said at last. "Be it on your own head.

"So long as it's no' on mine," he added. "Put your paws together, bend your knees, close your eyes, and take it steady. We're no want to start the day with a young bear's rupture."

Looking more and more surprised Paddington did as he was bidden. For a while all he could hear was a lot of grunting and groaning and he was about to stand up again when what seemed like a ton weight suddenly landed on his paws.

Opening his eyes in order to see what was going on he nearly fell over backwards with astonishment. Or rather, he would have fallen over if his paws hadn't been pinned to the ground by what appeared to be an enormous telegraph pole.

But if the whole thing looked frightening at first sight it was nothing compared to the situation a few seconds later when he heaved the pole in the air in order to try and free himself.

For a brief moment all was well and a ripple of applause ran round the assembly, but almost at once things started to go wrong.

Hearing the cries of alarm as the pole began to fall Paddington hurried after it as fast as he could, only to feel it start to topple in the opposite direction.

The man in charge jumped back. "Och aye!" he shouted. "Take it away—it's all yours!"

"I don't think I want it any more, thank you very much," gasped Paddington, turning to the speaker.

But it was too late. The man had disappeared and

instead words of advice and encouragement began to rain on him from all sides.

"Watch out!"

"Brace yourself!"

"Left paw down a bit!"

There were so many different instructions he couldn't even begin to remember half of them let alone decide which one to act on first.

He would have liked very much to give the pole away to someone but as fast as he ran with it in one direction the crowd scattered in the other.

It was all like some terrible nightmare, or rather all the nightmares he had ever known rolled into one, with the pictures flitting back and forth across his vision like some gigantic television screen that had gone wildly out of control.

And then, just as he was beginning to give up all hope of ever being saved, he heard a familiar voice rising above the others.

"Over here, Mr. Brown!" shouted Mr. Gruber. "Over here!"

Like a drowning man clutching at a straw Paddington closed his eyes, heaved the pole for all it was worth, and then let go.

He wasn't quite sure what happened next. For an instant everything went black and the whole world seemed to turn upside down, then there was a tremendous thud and a clang followed by silence.

"Oh dear, Mr. Brown," said a voice, as a willing pair

of hands helped him to his feet. "I'm afraid this is all my fault. If I hadn't called you when I did it would never have happened."

Paddington opened his eyes and stared round in alarm, but to his relief Mr. Gruber's car still seemed to be in one piece.

"It's a good job the pole hit this wheel and not the car itself," said Mr. Gruber, picking up a twisted piece of metal, "otherwise it really would have been an 'old crock'. But I'm very much afraid it's put paid to our chances of entering the Grand Parade," he added ruefully.

Paddington's face grew longer and longer as he took in Mr. Gruber's words. "Perhaps we could trying running it on *three* wheels?" he suggested hopefully.

Mr. Gruber shook his head. "It's been known," he said. "In fact, I do believe there's someone who holds the record for running a car on *two* wheels, but we would need a very large weight on the back seat to balance things up and I doubt if we'll get one in time. Jonathan and Judy certainly won't be heavy enough and there's only ten minutes to go before the start . . ."

Mr. Gruber broke off, for much to his surprise his words seemed to be having a strange effect.

One moment Paddington was standing in front of him forlornly eyeing the squashed remains of the wheel, the next moment he was galvanized into action rather as if he'd suddenly received an electric shock.

"I shan't be a moment, Mr. Gruber," he called. "I've just had an idea!" And before Mr. Gruber had time to open his mouth, let alone reply, he'd disappeared into the crowd with a very determined expression on his face indeed.

Despite his friend's assurances on the matter Paddington still felt most upset about his unfortunate accident. He was anxious to make amends and Mr. Gruber's remark about needing a large weight in a hurry had triggered off an idea in the back of his mind.

The object of Paddington's attention was a large stage which lay towards the back of the Fair. However, it wasn't so much the stage or the ropes surrounding it that had set his mind to work, but a large poster hanging overhead. It was labelled TWO-TON "MUSCLES" GALORE and it showed a view of the largest man he could ever remember seeing.

Paddington didn't know what "Muscles" Galore did

for a living or why he was at the Fair, but if his picture was anything to go by and he sat in the back of Mr. Gruber's car there would be no possibility whatsoever of it ever falling over.

As he climbed through the ropes on to the stage Paddington was surprised to hear a cheer ring out and he paused for a moment in order to raise his hat at the crowd below before hurrying across to the far corner where a man in leopard-skin tights was sitting.

"Excuse me, Mr. Galore," he began, politely holding out his paw. "I was wondering . . ."

The rest of Paddington's words died before they even reached his lips.

He wasn't quite sure how it happened or why for that matter, but somewhere a bell clanged and he suddenly found himself flying through the air towards the ropes on the far side of the stage almost as if he'd been shot from a cannon. It felt like a ride on a helter-skelter, a moon-rocket, and a dodg'em car all rolled into one, and to his alarm no sooner had he recovered from his first shock than he caught sight of "Muscles" Galore advancing towards him again with a most unfriendly look in his eye.

"Would like a second?" whispered a hoarse voice in his ear.

Paddington looked round and found he was being addressed by a man with a towel round his neck. "I didn't even want the first, thank you very much," he said hotly.

"If you want my advice," said the man, "you'll go in there fighting and give him 'what for' while you've got the chance. I should watch it though, he's got a chip on his shoulder."

"Mr. Galore's got a chip on his shoulder?" repeated Paddington, licking his lips. Although he didn't think much of his new friend's advice he found the last piece of information much more to his liking. All the activity that morning had made him feel hungry and he peered hopefully at the advancing figure.

But his interest was short-lived. There wasn't so much as a potato peeling on Mr. Galore's shoulders let alone any chips, and as he loomed nearer and nearer, snorting and baring his teeth, it was all too easy to see how he'd earned his name. In fact, he seemed to have muscles on top of his muscles and Paddington didn't like the look of the way some of them were rippling at all.

"Lay in to 'im!" shouted someone in the crowd. "Tear 'im apart!"

Paddington wasn't sure whether the remark was intended for him or Two-Ton "Muscles" Galore, but he didn't stop to find out. Pulling his hat firmly down over his head he slithered past his opponent and hurried round the ring in an effort to find the nearest exit. He was only just in the nick of time for there was a loud "twang" behind him as "Muscles" Galore landed against the ropes and bounced off again, landing with a heavy thud on the floor.

The roar which greeted Paddington's narrow escape

was equalled only by the growl from Two-Ton Muscles as his outstretched hands grasped at the empty air.

"First rate," said someone, pushing Paddington back into the ring as he tried to clamber through the ropes. "I don't think I'd want to stay in the ring with a great brute like that just for the sake of a pound a minute."

"Not for fifty pounds," agreed someone else. "I'd like to live to spend it. Still, it's the best so far today. By my reckoning that young bear's two quid up already."

Paddington stared at the speaker in amazement. Far from wanting to earn a pound for every minute spent in

the ring with "Muscles" Galore, he would willingly have forgone quite a few weeks' bun money in order to stay out.

But before he had time to think too deeply about the matter he felt a vice-like grip encircle his waist and for a second time in as many minutes he found himself hurtling through the air.

"'Ere!" called "Muscles" Galore, as he staggered back against the ropes. "'E's all slippery. He's coated 'isself with something."

"Get on with it!" shouted someone in the crowd.

Two-ton "Muscles" Galore turned and glared at the audience. "I can't fight 'im," he yelled. "It's like trying to wrestle with a pussy-cat."

"Meeow," called a voice, as the crowd dissolved into laughter. "Meeeow."

"Puss, puss, puss," echoed more voices as they took up the cry.

The chanting of the crowd seemed to act like a red rag to a bull on "Muscles" Galore and for the next few minutes Paddington was hard put to keep ahead of him let alone make good his escape from the ring as they tore round and round.

How long it would have gone on was impossible to say, for as fast as Two-Ton "Muscles" Galore caught up with Paddington and grabbed hold of him he slipped from his grasp again, and it was really more a question of who would hold out the longest.

But as it happened matters were suddenly decided

for them in the shape of a stern figure emerging from the crowd brandishing an umbrella.

Ignoring the boos from the rougher element who would willingly have seen the contest go on all day, Mrs. Bird climbed into the ring.

"Stop these 'goings-on' at once!" she commanded, glaring at Paddington's opponent. "'Muscles' Galore indeed! You ought to be ashamed of yourself—chasing a young bear like that!"

"It wasn't really Mr. Galore's fault, Mrs. Bird," gasped Paddington urgently. "And it wasn't his muscles I was after—it was his tons!"

With only seconds to go before the start of the Grand Parade Paddington wasn't at all sure if he could get Two-Ton "Muscles" Galore to the car in time let alone explain why he wanted him.

He gave a deep sigh as he tried to gather his breath. "If you like to come and sit on Mr. Gruber's back seat, Mr. Galore," he announced generously, "I'll give you back my winnings!"

Two-Ton "Muscles" Galore needed no second bidding. In fact, he looked quite pleased to leave the ring, and a moment later, with Paddington leading and Mrs. Bird bringing up the rear, they were pushing their way through the crowd in the direction of Mr. Gruber's car as fast as they could go.

After all the excitement the events which followed— even the strange sight of Mr. Gruber's "old crock" heading the procession on three wheels, its bonnet adorned by an enormous blue "winner's" rosette and the back seat by the equally huge figure of Mr. Galore— proved something of an anti-climax.

Both Paddington and Mr. Gruber were well-known figures in the market and it was a popular result, but long after the Parade was over and the last of the Fair was being packed up ready to leave, the main talking point was Paddington's exploits in the ring.

Even "Muscles" Galore himself made a special point of shaking him warmly by the paw before he left.

"Such a nice gentleman," said Mrs. Bird surprisingly, as she waved goodbye.

"Quite one of the old school," agreed Mr. Gruber. "I think he and young Mr. Brown were very well matched. With odds-on Mr. Brown, of course," he added hastily.

"Fancy staying in the ring with him for *ten* whole minutes though," exclaimed Jonathan admiringly. "I wouldn't have fancied it."

"The man who ran the booth announced it was a record," broke in Judy.

"Mr. Galore said I'm what they call a South Paw," explained Paddington. "That's most unusual."

The Browns exchanged glances. There was a peculiar gleam in Paddington's eye and it was noticeable that they were being given an extra wide berth by the other passers-by as they made their way home.

"I must say it's nice to feel in such safe paws," said

74

Mrs. Bird, as Paddington aimed a particularly hard stare at a nearby shadow. "Especially late at night."

"What are you going to do when you get home, Paddington?" asked Mr. Brown jokingly. "Have half an hour with a medicine ball or do some press-ups?"

Paddington directed his stare in Mr. Brown's direction. "I think," he said, to everyone's astonishment, "I shall have a nice hot bath."

"Good gracious!" exclaimed Mrs. Brown. "Wonders will never cease."

But Paddington had other things on his mind. Thinking back over the day's events he'd decided that the thing that had impressed him most of all was the outcome of the previous night's bubble bath. The result of only a few capfuls had surpassed anything forecast on the side of the jar and there was no knowing what might happen if he used the rest in one go.

"My fur's got very dusty, Mr. Brown," he announced hopefully, "so I think I shall need plenty of your mixture to put it right!"

CHAPTER FIVE

The Case of the Doubtful Dummy

Mr. Brown lowered his evening newspaper and glanced up at the dining-room ceiling as a strange wailing sound, half-human – half-animal, rang out from somewhere overhead.

"What on earth was that?" he asked.

"It's only Paddington," replied Mrs. Brown soothingly. "I let him borrow Jonathan's old violin to play with. I expect he's got caught up in the strings again. It's a bit difficult with paws."

"Jonathan's old violin?" repeated Mr. Brown. "It sounds more like someone putting a cat through a mangle!" He gave a shiver as another banshee-like note echoed round the house. "Don't tell me he's taking up music now."

"I don't think so, Henry," replied Mrs. Brown vaguely. "He said it had something to do with his detective work."

"Oh, Lord!" Mr. Brown gave a groan as he settled back in his arm-chair. "Well, I wish he would hurry up and solve something. Perhaps we shall have a bit of peace and quiet then."

"At least it keeps him out of mischief," said Mrs. Brown.

Mrs. Bird looked up from her knitting. "It all depends on what you mean by mischief," she said meaningly. "If you ask me it's more eating than detecting. I caught him looking for clues in my larder this morning."

The Browns' housekeeper tended to view most of Paddington's activities with suspicion and his latest one was no exception. Indeed, when he'd finally emerged from the larder his face had worn an unusually guilty expression for someone who was supposed to be on the side of law and order.

Paddington's interest in detective work had started several weeks earlier when he'd had to spend some time in bed.

Shortly after the Fair the fortune-teller's warning had come true and he'd caught a cold. It had been a particularly nasty one; for a while he'd been completely off marmalade sandwiches—always a sure sign that things were not as they should be, and when the worst was over Mrs. Bird had insisted on his staying indoors for a few extra days just to be on the safe side.

With Jonathan and Judy back at school, Mrs. Brown had been hard put to keep him amused and in desperation she'd lent him some of her husband's library books. Mr. Brown liked detective stories and in no time at all Paddington began to share his enthusiasm. Even though he was a slow reader he managed to get through quite a number and after some discussion with the local librarian Mrs. Brown made arrangements for him to have his own ticket for a trial period.

From that moment on Paddington visited the library several times a week and he soon became quite a familiar figure in the "mystery" section.

One of his favourite characters was a private detective called Carlton Dale—partly because his books were on the bottom shelf and easy to get at and partly because there seemed to be a never-ending supply. Mr. Dale solved many of his cases from the comfort of his own home and—like Sherlock Holmes before him—he often soothed his nerves with the aid of a violin. In fact, he seemed to spend most of his time sitting up in bed playing selections from *The Desert Song* while baffled officials from Scotland Yard sought his advice on their latest unsolved case.

Unaware of the disturbance he was causing downstairs, Paddington pushed the bow back and forth over his own instrument several times and then gloomily laid it down on his bedside table. He had to admit that the noise was far from soothing, particularly as he hadn't even got a case to work on.

In the books Carlton Dale was never short of cases. If it wasn't the milkman falling down dead on his door-step it was someone from the police knocking him up with some urgent problem or other.

Peering out of the front room window early one morning Paddington came to the conclusion that the Browns' milkman looked unusually healthy, and when he tried ringing up the local police station to see if they had any unsolved crimes they were most unhelpful.

Heaving a deep sigh he turned his attention to a letter he'd just finished writing. It was addressed to Mr. Carlton Dale himself and in it Paddington had sought advice on how to look for cases.

According to his books, Carlton Dale lived in a fashion-able quarter of London and Paddington felt sure that he must be well known to the Post Office, particularly as he'd once solved THE CASE OF THE MISSING MAILBAGS for them.

Carefully sealing the envelope, he inscribed Mr. Dale's name on the outside, donned his duffle-coat and hat, and then made his way downstairs in order to borrow a stamp.

"Oh, dear," said Mrs. Brown anxiously, when she saw what he was up to. "*Must* it go tonight?" She lifted one of the curtains and peered into the gloom. "It's a thick fog. Not fit for a dog to be out, let alone a bear. I think *you'd* better go, Henry."

"Thank you very much," said Mr. Brown from behind his paper. "I've had quite enough fog for one night driving home—without posting bears' letters."

"It's all right, Mrs. Brown," broke in Paddington hastily. "I'd rather do it myself, thank you." And before the others had a chance to open their mouths he'd disappeared out of the dining-room.

To be truthful Paddington didn't really want anyone else to see who he'd been writing to and he was in so much of a hurry to escape it wasn't until the front door closed behind him that he began to have second thoughts on the matter. For if it had looked murky through the Browns' dining-room window it seemed doubly so now he was outside.

Pulling the duffle-coat hood over his hat he wrapped a handkerchief round his nose in order to keep out the worst of the smog, and after taking a deep breath began edging his way carefully along Windsor Gardens towards the pillar-box at the far end.

Paddington had never been out in a really thick fog before and it wasn't long before he made a strange discovery. The railings which he'd been carefully keeping on his right had suddenly disappeared, and although he must have trodden the same path countless times in the past he hadn't the slightest idea where he was.

Worse still, when he turned round in what he thought was a half circle in order to retrace his steps, he walked headlong into a tree, which certainly hadn't been there on his way out.

Paddington was a brave bear at heart but he began to grow more and more anxious as he groped his way along and not a single familiar landmark came into view.

Even the roads were strangely silent, with only the occasional outline of an abandoned car or other vehicle to show they were there at all, and as time went by with no sign of any passer-by to advise him he had to admit that he was well and truly lost.

He tried calling out "Help!" several times, first fairly quietly and then in a much louder voice, but it had no effect at all. Indeed, for all the good it did he might just as well have saved his breath.

Lowering the handkerchief from his nose Paddington

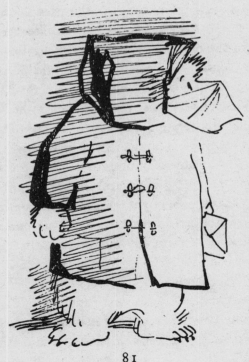

felt under his hat, removed the marmalade sandwich he always kept there in case of an emergency, and was just about to sit down in order to consider his next move when he gradually became aware of a faint glow somewhere ahead of him.

Like a light-house beam to a lost mariner, the glimmer gave him fresh heart and in no time at all he was making all haste in its direction.

The light seemed to be coming from a building with a number of very large windows and as he drew near Paddington suddenly recognised it as a large department store he'd visited many times in the past. How he'd got there he didn't know, for it lay in quite the opposite direction to the one he'd expected. But having found his bearings at long last he felt sure he would be able to get home again simply by following a main road which ran near to Windsor Gardens. Indeed, even as he stood considering the matter, he distinctly caught the welcome sound of slow-moving traffic in the distance.

There was a lady standing in one of the windows, peering out into the gloom, and he was about to tap on the glass and ask where the nearest bus stop was when he suddenly stopped in his tracks, the marmalade sandwich poised halfway to his mouth and all thoughts of returning home momentarily forgotten.

Pulling the handkerchief over his face, Paddington stepped back a pace into the mist and then watched with ever-growing astonishment as a man with a beard crept through a door at the back of the window, and threw a white sheet over the lady. Before she had time to cry out let alone put up any kind of a struggle, he picked her bodily up and then crept out again, closing the door behind him in what could only be described as an extremely furtive manner indeed.

It was all over in a matter of seconds and Paddington could hardly believe his eyes. It was THE CASE OF THE MISERABLE MUMMIES all over again, only more so because he'd actually seen it happen with his own eyes.

In the book of that name Carlton Dale had solved a particularly dastardly crime to do with kidnapping in which the unfortunate victims had been hypnotised and then left in a shop window disguised as dummies to await collection during the night.

The likeness of the two stories was uncanny, even down to the fog and the man with the beard. Most of the crimes in Carlton Dale's casebook took place under cover of a thick fog—when the police were powerless to act, and a great many of them were committed by men with beards. Indeed, Carlton Dale himself seemed fascinated by beards of any sort, and he was forever pulling them off on the final page in order to unmask the true villain.

Mr. Dale had solved THE CASE OF THE MISERABLE MUMMIES by taking on a job in the store itself, and if Paddington had entertained any thoughts about reporting his strange experience to the police they disappeared for good and all a moment later when he caught sight of a notice pasted to one of the shop windows near the main entrance. It said, simply: VACANCIES. GOOD

PROSPECTS. OWN CANTEEN. APPLY MISS GLORIA.
STAFF APPOINTMENTS.

It was unusually late before Paddington finally turned
out his bedside light that night, and even then he was
much too excited to sleep.

Once or twice he switched it back on again in order
to make an entry on a large sheet of paper headed
"CLEWS", and it needed several quite long sessions on
his violin before he finally dropped off to sleep.

Fortunately, the Browns were so thankful he'd arrived
home safely after his long absence they managed to turn
a deaf ear, but on the last two occasions Mr. Curry was
heard to fling open his bedroom window and empty a jug
of water into the garden below. And if the tone of his
voice was anything to go by any Tom cat who happened
to be passing at the time would have been well advised
to turn back without delay.

However, despite his late night, Paddington woke
early next morning. When he drew his curtains he was
pleased to see the fog had almost cleared and after a
quick wash, followed by an even quicker breakfast, he
got ready to depart again.

"I do wish I could see into Paddington's mind," said
Mrs. Brown, as the front door closed behind him. "I
know something's going on. I can recognise the signs.
Besides, it's bonfire night at the week-end and there was
a letter from Jonathan this morning asking him to see
about the fireworks. He hasn't done a thing yet. It's most
unusual."

"If you ask me," said Mrs. Bird, "it's a good job we *can't* see into that bear's mind. There's no knowing what we might find sometimes!"

Despite her words the Browns' housekeeper looked as if she would have liked to ask Paddington a few questions as well, but by that time he was much too far away, and busy with problems of his own.

It took him some while to find the Appointments Office of the store where the mysterious goings-on had taken place the night before, and as he approached a lady sitting behind a desk at the far end of the room a clock was already striking ten somewhere in the distance.

"Excuse me, Miss Gloria," he announced urgently, "I've come about the job in the window. I'd like to be taken on, please."

The lady in charge of appointments appeared to have problems of her own, for she carried on writing. "Are you an 'under a thousand pounds a year man'?" she asked briefly.

"Oh, yes," said Paddington eagerly. "I'm a one and sixpence a week bear."

"A one and sixpence a week *bear*?" Miss Gloria gave a start as she glanced up from her work.

"I don't think you're quite what we're looking for," she began, breaking off as Paddington fixed her with a hard stare.

"Er . . . have you tried the Post Office?" she asked, in a slightly more helpful tone. "Perhaps you could put your name down as a Christmas 'temp'."

"A Christmas 'temp'?" repeated Paddington hotly. "I don't want to work for the Post Office—I want to work for you. It's a matter of life and death!"

"Oh, really?" Miss Gloria's expression changed and she began to look quite flustered. "Er... how nice. I... er... I'd like to help you," she continued, patting her hair, "but I don't think I can put you behind a counter. You may have trouble seeing over the top. After all, you are rather . . . er . . ." Once again her voice trailed away as she caught Paddington's gaze. "I really don't think I can offer you anything in the way of a *four*-figure job," she said unhappily, rifling through some cards.

"Have you a three-figure one?" asked Paddington hopefully.

Miss Gloria paused and withdrew a card from the file. "There *is* one here," she said. "And I suppose you *could* call it a three-figure job. It's three pounds ten a week, actually, and we *do* supply a free mackintosh."

"A free mackintosh?" repeated Paddington, becoming more and more surprised. "Isn't the job inside?"

"Well," said Miss Gloria uneasily. "It is and it isn't. Most of you is under cover. You'd be in charge of our sandwich board, actually."

Paddington's eyes glistened. It seemed even better than he'd dared hope for. "Do I bring my own sandwiches?" he inquired, "or do you supply them?"

Miss Gloria gave a shrill laugh. "I'll give you a chit," she said hurriedly. "You'd better go down and see our Mr. Waters. He's in charge of the stores and he'll fit you out. That is, if you want the job?"

"Oh, yes, please," said Paddington. He'd never been in charge of any sort of board before, let alone a sandwich one at three pounds ten a week, and after thanking the lady very much for all her trouble he hurried back downstairs as fast as he could.

The storeman eyed Paddington gloomily as he examined the chit. "I suppose they 'as to take what they can get these days," he said. "But I shouldn't go joining no pension scheme if I were you. I doubt if you'll last that long!"

Mr. Waters disappeared behind some metal racks for a moment or two and when he returned he was staggering beneath a pile of what looked like old tables with advertisement slogans painted on them.

"Try this on for size," he said, lifting the conglomeration over Paddington's head. "'Ave a walk up and down and get the feel of it."

Paddington peered at the storeman over the top of his board as if in a trance. Far from needing to walk up and down he knew just what it felt like without even moving.

"What do you think?" asked Mr. Waters. "I don't know as we 'as a smaller one."

Paddington took a deep breath. His hat had been pushed down over his head; his whiskers were ruffled; and to make matters worse the straps were biting into his shoulders as if he was supporting a ton weight.

He was about to tell the storeman exactly what he thought about sandwich boards in general and the one belonging to the store in particular when he suddenly froze, hardly able to believe his good fortune. For a new figure had come into view through the door. Or rather, not a new figure, but an all too familiar one with a beard.

"Hallo, 'Soapy'!" The newcomer nodded towards the back of the store as he addressed Mr. Waters. "You've still got 'you know who' all right?"

The storeman gave a wink. "She 'asn't moved, Mr. Adrian," he chuckled. "Snug as a bug in a rug. All right for the week-end, eh? No change of plans?"

The man with the beard nodded again. "There's a whole gang coming," he said. "Can't stop now. My turn to get the coffee this morning—all twenty-three! Just thought I'd check on my way to the canteen."

Paddington stood rooted to the spot as the voices died away. It hadn't occurred to him that he might have a gang to deal with. It was THE CASE OF THE DOZEN DESPERADOES all over again, only with eleven extra members, and it took him some moments to digest this new piece of information.

"I 'as to lock up now," said the storeman, breaking into his thoughts as he came back into the room. "It's coffee time. If you want my advice you'll get a cuppa while you've got the chance. It's thirsty work lugging sandwich boards about. The canteen's just along on your right. Follow Mr. Adrian—you can't miss it."

But Mr. Waters was addressing the empty air, for Paddington was already clumping his way along the corridor in hot pursuit of his suspect.

Regardless of the queer looks being cast in his direction, he pushed his way into the canteen past a row of startled onlookers and made his way along the front of the counter until he was right behind the man with the beard.

Although Carlton Dale had never mentioned having to wear a sandwich board on any of his cases, Paddington was glad he hadn't stopped to remove it, for at least it gave him cover while he considered his next move.

Peering over the top he racked his brains as the man in front loaded a tray with cups and saucers and then felt in a purse for the money.

It was as the lady behind the cash register handed over the change and slammed the till shut that Paddington had a sudden flash of inspiration; for the sight of all the money reminded him of yet another of Mr. Dale's famous cases—THE AFFAIR OF THE FORGED FLORINS—in which the criminal had been tracked down with the aid of fingerprints taken from the coins themselves.

"Excuse me," he called, addressing the lady behind the counter. "Have you seen what's on the wall behind you?"

As the cashier looked round Paddington seized his opportunity. Reaching out from beneath the board he hastily turned the cash register round until it was facing him and then pressed one of the buttons.

He wasn't at all sure what happened next, for it was all over before he had time to blink, let alone see inside the till. There was a "ping" as the drawer shot out, and a split second later a crash echoed and re-echoed round the canteen as twenty-three cups of coffee went flying in all directions.

"Mr. Adrian! Mr. Adrian!" The lady behind the cash desk peered under the counter as a cry of mingled pain and astonishment came from somewhere underneath. "Are you all right?"

"What a thing to happen," she cried, turning to one of the assistants. "And only two days before Bonfire Night!"

"He's been to so much trouble and all," clucked some-one else. "They say he's made a marvellous guy from a dummy out of one of his windows. Been keeping it down in the stores as a surprise."

"He did it!" shouted another assistant, pointing at Paddington. "The one with the whiskers behind that sandwich board. He did it on purpose."

"I knew he was up to no good as soon as he came in," cried a waitress. "He pushed me in my vanilla slices he was in such a hurry!"

"Help! Bandits!" shouted yet another voice, taking up the call.

Immediately the whole canteen was in an uproar as attention suddenly switched from the unfortunate Mr. Adrian, still lying under the counter in a pool of brown liquid, and focused on the sandwich board.

But Paddington was no longer inside it. Like Carlton Dale at his most elusive, he had disappeared. He still hadn't had time to take in all that had been said, but of one thing he was perfectly certain; any working out of the problem which remained was much better done in the quiet of number thirty-two Windsor Gardens rather than the store's canteen.

"There's a funny case in tonight's paper," said Mr.

Brown, later that same evening. "Quite near here. Apparently they had some sort of to-do in that big store.

"'Sandwich-board runs amok in staff canteen,'" he read. "'Bearded window-dresser attacked by mystery coffee-throwing bandit!'"

"What will people get up to next?" asked Mrs. Brown, from behind her knitting. "You're not safe anywhere these days."

Mr. Brown tossed the paper on to the floor for the others to see. "Sounds like a case for you, Paddington," he called jokingly. "I bet you five pounds you can't solve that one!"

Paddington, who'd spent most of the evening busily writing notes in his scrap-book, nearly fell off the pouffe with astonishment.

"Would you really, Mr. Brown?" he exclaimed excitedly.

"Er...yes," replied Mr. Brown, suddenly looking slightly less enthusiastic about the matter. "That's what I said."

There was a confident note to Paddington's voice he didn't entirely like the sound of, and he looked even more unhappy a moment or so later when Paddington cut a picture out of the paper and began pasting it alongside his notes.

"Don't tell me you've been working on the case already?" he asked.

Paddington nodded as he licked a gummed label to place under the photograph of a coffee-stained Mr.

Adrian being interviewed with his guy. He suddenly felt very much better about everything. Carlton Dale rarely received any sort of reward for solving *his* crimes, let alone five pounds, and although he didn't think he could possibly make as good a guy as the one in the picture he was quite certain Mr. Brown's money would go a long way towards it, and supply a goodly number of extra fireworks for Jonathan and Judy into the bargain.

"I've called it THE CASE OF THE DOUBTFUL DUMMY," he announced importantly, clearing his throat as everyone gathered round to listen. "It all began yesterday evening when I wrote to Carlton Dale . . ."

CHAPTER SIX

Paddington Recommended

Mrs. Brown tore open the first of the morning's mail, withdrew a large piece of white pasteboard, and then stared at it in amazement. "Good gracious!" she exclaimed. "Fancy that! Mrs. Smith-Cholmley is holding a Christmas ball in aid of the local children's hospital and we've all been invited."

Paddington peered across the table with a slice of toast and marmalade poised halfway to his mouth. "Mrs. Smith-Cholmley's holding a Christmas ball?" he repeated in great surprise. "I hope we get there before she drops it!"

"It isn't that sort of a ball, dear," said Mrs. Brown patiently.

"It means she's having a dance," explained Judy.

"Who's Mrs. Smith-Cholmley when she's at home?" asked Mr. Brown.

Mrs. Brown handed him the card. "Don't you re-member, Henry? Paddington met her when he was out Carol Singing last year. She's the one he cooked the baked elastic for by mistake."

"Crikey!" broke in Jonathan, as he read the invitation. "She's either left it a bit late or it's been delayed in the post. It's tomorrow night!"

"And that's not all," added Mrs. Brown. "Have you seen what it says at the bottom?"

Paddington hurried round the table and peered over Mr. Brown's shoulder. "Ruzzvup!" he exclaimed.

"No, dear," said Mrs. Brown. "R.S.V.P. That simply means '*Répondez, s'il vous plâit*'. It's French for 'please reply'."

"You mean the bit about evening dress?" Mr. Brown looked round at Paddington, who was waving his toast and marmalade dangerously near his left ear. "Well, that's put the tin lid on it. I suppose we shall just have to say no."

There was a note of relief in Mr. Brown's voice. He wasn't too keen on dancing at the best of times and the thought of going to a ball run by Mrs. Smith-Cholmley filled him with gloom. But any hopes he'd entertained of using Paddington as an excuse were quickly dashed by the chorus of dismay which greeted his last remark.

"I think we ought to try and arrange *something*, Henry," said Mrs. Brown. "After all, it's in a very good cause. It's the same hospital Paddington collected for last year, and if it wasn't for him we shouldn't be invited anyway."

"We'll take him along to Heather and Sons and have him fitted out for the evening," said Mrs. Bird decidedly, as she bustled around clearing up the breakfast things. "They hire out evening clothes and it says in their advertisements they fit anyone while they wait."

Mr. Brown eyed Paddington's figure doubtfully. "We need it *tomorrow* night," he said. "Not next year."

Paddington looked most upset at this last remark. It was bad enough writing things in initials, let alone French ones, but having to wear special clothes simply in order to dance seemed most complicated.

However, he brightened considerably at the thought of going up to London to be fitted out. And when Mr. Brown, recognising defeat at last, announced that he would meet them afterwards and take them all out to lunch as a special treat he joined in the general excitement.

Paddington liked visiting London and he couldn't wait to get started, especially when Mr. Brown brought out his copy of a guide to good restaurants and began searching for a likely eating place.

"They have a restaurant at Heather's now," said Mrs. Brown. "We could combine the two things. It'll save a lot of trouble."

Mr. Brown made a quick check. "It isn't a Duncan Hyde recommended," he said disappointedly. "He doesn't even mention it."

"It only opened last week," replied Mrs. Brown, "so it wouldn't be. But not many people know about it yet so at least it won't be crowded."

"All right," said Mr. Brown. "You win!" He snapped the book shut and handed it to Paddington. "Perhaps you can test a few of the dishes at lunchtime," he continued, as the others hurried upstairs. "If they're any good we'll send a recommendation to Mr. Hyde."

"Thank you very much, Mr. Brown," said Paddington gratefully. He'd spent many happy hours browsing through the pages of Mr. Hyde's book and he put it away carefully in the secret compartment of his suitcase while he got ready to go out.

Duncan Hyde spent his time visiting restaurants all over the country, awarding them various shaped hats for their cooking, ranging from a very small beret for run-of-the-mill dishes to a giant size bowler for the very best, and some of the dishes he described were mouth-watering indeed.

Although no one had ever met him, for he preferred to remain anonymous, it was widely agreed that he must be a person of great taste, and when they arrived at Heather and Sons later that morning Paddington peered through the restaurant window with interest in case there was anyone around carrying a hat.

As they trooped through the main entrance the Browns were greeted by a man in morning dress.

"We'd like to fit this young bear out for a special occasion," said Mrs. Brown. "Can you direct us to the right department, please?"

"Certainly, Modom. Please step this way." With scarcely the flicker of an eyelid the supervisor turned

and led the way towards a nearby lift. "Is the young
... er, gentleman, being presented at Court?" he asked,
glancing down at Paddington as the doors slid shut.
"Or is he simply coming out?"

"Neither," said Paddington, giving the man a hard
stare. "I'm coming in!" After the warmth of the under-
ground the air outside had struck particularly cold to his
whiskers and he didn't want to be sent out again.

"He's going to a ball," explained Mrs. Brown hastily.
"We want to hire some evening dress."

"A ball?" The man looked slightly relieved. "One of
the Spring functions, no doubt?" he remarked hopefully.

"No," said Mrs. Bird firmly. "One of the Christmas
ones. It's for tomorrow night, so there's no time to be
lost."

"It says in the advertisement you fit anyone," broke
in Jonathan.

"While you wait," added Judy imploringly.

"Er ... yes," said the supervisor unhappily. He looked
down at Paddington again. "It's just that the young
... er ... gentleman's legs are a bit ... ahem ... and we
may have to do some rather drastic alterations if it's to be
from stock."

"My legs are a bit 'ahem'?" exclaimed Paddington
hotly.

He began giving the supervisor some very hard stares
indeed, but fortunately the lift came to a stop before any
more could be said. As the doors slid open and the man
gave a discreet signal to an assistant hovering in the back-

ground, Mrs. Brown exchanged glances with the others.

"I was wondering," she said, "if it wouldn't be better for the rest of us to carry on with our Christmas shopping? We can all meet again in the restaurant downstairs at one o'clock."

"A very good idea, Modom!" The supervisor sounded most relieved. "Rest assured," he continued, as he ushered Paddington from the lift, "we will use our best endeavours and leave no stone unturned. I'll get our Mr. Stanley to look after the young gentleman. He does all our difficult cases and there's nothing he likes better than a challenge."

"That's as may be," said Mrs. Bird ominously, as the gates slid shut again, "but I have a feeling he's going to have to turn over a good few stones before that bear's fitted out. You mark my words!"

The Browns' housekeeper didn't entirely approve of leaving Paddington to the tender mercies of Heather and Sons, impressive though their shop was, but as it happened the supervisor's confidence in his staff was not misplaced, for no sooner had the Browns departed than everyone sprang into action.

"I'll put 'Thimbles' Martin on the job," announced Mr. Stanley, making notes as he circled Paddington with a tape measure. "He's the fastest man with a needle and thread in the business. He'll fix you up in no time at all."

Looking suitably impressed Paddington settled down to read his Duncan Hyde book while he waited, and indeed, it seemed only a very short while before Mr. Stanley reappeared proudly carrying an immaculately pressed set of evening clothes.

"You'll look a blade in these and no mistake, sir," he exclaimed enthusiastically, as he led Paddington into a changing cubicle.

"Quite the young bear about town," agreed the supervisor. "Mind you," he continued, allowing himself a smile of satisfaction as he helped Paddington on with the jacket, "you'll have to watch your P's and Q's. There's no knowing who you might not get mistaken for dressed like that. Will you be taking them with you, or shall we send them?"

Paddington examined his reflection in the mirror—or rather, since there were mirrors on all four walls, what seemed like a never-ending line of reflections stretching away into the distance.

Although he felt very pleased to get his evening dress so quickly he was looking forward even more to the thought of carrying out Mr. Brown's suggestion and investigating some dishes for the guide.

"I think," he announced at last, "I'll wear them, thank you very much." And disregarding the anxious expressions he was leaving behind he picked up his belongings and headed for the lift.

As Mrs. Brown had forecast, not many people knew about Heather's restaurant and what with that and the early hour it was still practically empty when Paddington entered.

Just inside the door there was an enormous sweet
trolley and his eyes nearly popped out with astonishment
as he took in the various items. There were so many
different shapes, sizes and colours he soon lost count, and
it was while he was on his paws and knees examining the
mounds of chocolate mousse and the oceans of fruit salads
on the bottom shelf that he suddenly realised someone
was talking to him.

"May I be of assistance?" asked one of the waiters.

Paddington stood up and raised his hat politely. "No,
thank you very much," he said sadly. "I was only looking." Holding up the Duncan Hyde book he ran his
eye over the trolley again. "I was hoping I might be able

to do some testing later on. I think some of your dishes might be worth a bowler."

To Paddington's surprise his words seemed to have a magical effect on the waiter. "Pardon me, sir," he exclaimed, jumping to attention. "I didn't realise who you were. If you care to wait just one moment, sir, I'll call the manager."

Bowing low as he backed away, the man disappeared from view, only to return a moment later accompanied by an imposing figure dressed in a black coat and striped trousers.

"I can't tell you," boomed the second man, rubbing his hands with invisible soap, "how delighted we are that you've decided to honour us with your presence. It's just what our restaurant needs." Taking in Paddington's dress suit, hat and whiskers he gave a knowing wink at the book. "I see you've been *hid*ing your light under a bushel!"

"I have?" exclaimed Paddington, looking more and more surprised at the turn the conversation was taking.

"We'll put you in the window, sir," announced the manager, leading the way across the floor. "We have some very special dishes on today," he confided with another wink, as he helped Paddington into a chair. "I'm sure we can find something to titivate your palate."

"I expect you can," said Paddington, politely giving the man a wink in return. "But I'm not sure if I can afford them."

"My dear sir," the man raised his hands in mock

horror as he whisked the menu away. "We don't want to bother ourselves with mere money."

"Don't we?" exclaimed Paddington excitedly.

The manager shook his head. "You need only sign the bill," he explained. "Let's think about food first. That's much more important. We want you to feel perfectly at home."

"Oh, I do already," said Paddington, grasping his knife and fork. "When can I start?"

"That's what I like to see," replied the manager— beaming all over his face. "Well," he continued, rubbing his hands in anticipation, "I can certainly recommend our avocado pear filled with sea-fresh prawns and cream sauce.

"After that," he said, "may I suggest either pot-fresh lobster, Dover-fresh sole, farm-fresh escalope of veal, or oven-fresh steak and kidney pudding?"

All the talk of food was beginning to make Paddington feel hungry and it didn't take him long to make up his mind. "I think I'd like to try some of each," he announced rashly.

If the manager was surprised he concealed his feelings remarkably well. In fact, a look of respect came over his face as he handed Paddington's order to a waiter who was hovering nearby. "I must say," he remarked, "you take your job very seriously, sir. There aren't many people in your position who would take the trouble to try *everything* on the menu. Would you care to test one of our rare old wines?"

Paddington thought for a moment. "I think I'd sooner test some of your tin-fresh cocoa," he said.

"Tin-fresh *cocoa?*" For one brief moment the manager's calm seemed to desert him, then he brightened. "I have a feeling you're trying to catch us out," he said, wagging his finger roguishly.

"Perhaps," he added, waving in the direction of the trolley, "you would care to contemplate the sweets over the cheese."

Paddington gave him an odd look. "I'd sooner eat them," he said. "But I think I'd better leave a little bit of room. I'm having lunch with someone at one o'clock."

A look of renewed admiration came over the man's face. "Well," he said, bowing his way out as the first of the dishes began to arrive, "I'll leave you to your task, but I do hope you'll see fit to mention us when the time comes."

"Oh, yes," replied Paddington earnestly. "I shall tell all my friends."

Paddington still wasn't sure wasn't sure why he was being treated in such a Royal manner, but he wasn't the sort of bear to look a gift horse in the mouth and as everyone obviously wanted him to enjoy his meal he was only too willing to oblige.

Already quite a large crowd had gathered on the pavement outside Heather's. In fact, the window was black with faces and it was getting darker with every passing moment.

Paddington's every move was watched with increasing

interest and as he settled down to his gargantuan meal
the applause which greeted each new course was exceeded
only by the one which followed.

But if the vast majority of the audience viewed the
goings-on inside the restaurant with wonder and delight,
there were five newly-joined members who stood watching
with horror and dismay on their faces.

The Browns had arranged to meet outside the shop,
but like most of the other passers-by they had been drawn
to the crowd gathered round the window, and now, as
they pushed their way through to the front, their worst
fears were realised.

"Mercy me!" cried Mrs. Bird. "What on earth is that
bear up to now?"

"I don't know what he's *up* to," said Mr. Brown gloomily, as a loud groan rose from the audience. "But whatever it is I think it's coming to an end."

A sudden change had indeed taken place on the other side of the glass, and the Browns watched with sinking hearts.

It all began when a waiter arrived bearing a large sheet of folded paper on a plate. Handing Paddington a pen he stood over him with a deferential smile on his face while he signed his name. Then gradually the smile disappeared, only to be replaced by an expression which the Browns didn't like the look of at all.

"Come on," cried Judy, grabbing her mother's arm. "We'd better do some rescuing."

"Oh, Lord!" groaned Mr. Brown, as they pushed their way back through the crowd. "Here we go again."

Unaware that help was on its way, Paddington stared at the waiter as if he could hardly believe his eyes let alone his ears. "Seven pounds sixteen shillings and four-pence!" he exclaimed. "Just for a meal?"

"Not just for *a* meal," said the waiter, eyeing all the stains. "About ten meals if you ask me. We thought you were Duncan Hyde, the famous gourmet."

Paddington nearly fell backwards off his chair at the news. "Duncan Hyde, the famous gourmet?" he repeated. "I'm not Duncan Hyde. I'm Paddington Brown from Darkest Peru and I'm a bear."

"In that case," said the waiter, handing back the bill,

"I'm afraid it's cash. It includes the 'cover-charge'," he added meaningly, "but not the tip."

"A *cover* charge?" exclaimed Paddington hotly. "But I didn't even have one. It was all open." He peered at the piece of paper in his paw. "*Seventeen shillings for a bombe surprise!*"

"That's all part of the surprise," replied the waiter nastily.

"Well, I've got one for you," said Paddington. "I've only got sixpence!"

Paddington felt most upset about the whole affair, especially as he hadn't intended eating in the first place. Apart from putting his signature on the bill as he'd been asked, he'd even added his special paw print to show it was genuine, and he looked very relieved when he caught sight of the Browns heading in his direction.

Since he'd arrived a great change had come over the restaurant and it was now full almost to overflowing. The Browns had to weave a tortuous path in and out of the other diners and before they were able to reach Paddington's table they found their way barred by the manager.

"Does this young gentleman belong to you?" he asked, pointing in Paddington's direction.

"Er . . . why do you ask?" queried Mr. Brown, playing for time.

"Henry!" exclaimed Mrs. Brown. "How could you?"

"I've never seen you before either, Mr. Brown," called Paddington, entering into the spirit of things.

Mr. Brown heaved a deep sigh as he reached for his wallet. "Since you ask," he said, "I'm afraid he does."

"Afraid?" The manager stared at the Browns. "Did you say *afraid*?" He waved an all-embracing hand round the restaurant. "Why, this is the best thing that's happened to us since we opened. That young bear's attracted so many new customers we don't know whether we're coming or going. There's certainly no charge."

He turned back to Paddington. "I wish we could have you sitting in the window every day of the week. You may not be a Duncan Hyde, but you're certainly worth yor weight in Lobster Soufflé . . ."

The manager broke off and looked at Paddington with concern. For some reason or other his words seemed to be having a strange effect.

"Are you all right, sir?" he asked. "Your whiskers seem to have gone a very funny colour. Let me help you up. Perhaps you'd like to try some of our bean-fresh coffee with cream?"

Paddington gave another groan. If he'd had to make a list of his needs at that moment, getting up would have figured very low while food and drink would have been lucky to get a mention at all.

Dropping his guide-book he sank back into the chair and felt for the buttons on his jacket. "I'd rather not do any more testing today, thank you very much," he gasped.

Apart from all his other troubles Paddington had noticed a rather ominous tearing sound whenever he moved, and although he'd minded his "peas" during lunch he had a feeling that both Mr. Stanley and "Thimbles" Martin were in for a busy afternoon dealing with his Q's.

All the same, he had to admit he'd never had *quite* such a meal in his life before.

"I think," he announced, "that if I was a food tester I would award Heather's one of my uncle's hats!"

Mr. Brown smacked his lips in anticipation. "It must be good then," he said, reaching for the menu. "I shall enjoy my lunch."

"After all," he continued, amid general agreement, "one of Paddington's hats must be worth a whole wardrobeful of Duncan Hyde bowlers any day of the week!"

CHAPTER SEVEN

The Last Dance

Mr. Brown hung his dressing-gown on the bedroom door and then sat on the bed rubbing his eyes. "Three times I've been down to the front door," he grumbled, "and all the time it was Paddington banging about in his room!"

"I expect he's practising his dancing," said Mrs. Brown sleepily. "He said he was having trouble with his turns last night."

"Well, I'm having trouble with my *sleep* this morning," said Mr. Brown crossly. "I've put my foot down."

"I can see you have," replied Mrs. Brown, eyeing her husband's slippers as he took them off. "Right in the middle of Paddington's rosin! I think you'd better scrape it off. He'll be most upset if there's any missing. He bought it specially to stop his paws slipping on the linoleum. He had several nasty falls yesterday."

Mr. Brown looked at his soles in disgust. "Only a bear," he said bitterly, "would want to do the tango at half past six on a Saturday morning. I only hope they don't have a 'bear's excuse me' at the ball tonight. Anyone who lands Paddington as a partner is in for a pretty rough time."

"Perhaps he'll have improved by then," said Mrs. Brown hopefully. "It can't be easy rehearsing with a bolster."

Mrs. Brown turned over and closed her eyes, though more in an effort to blot out the mental picture of events to come than with any hope of going back to sleep. For although one half of her was looking forward to Mrs. Smith-Cholmley's ball that evening, the other half was beginning to have grave doubts about the matter, and recent events only served to tip the scales still further on the side of the doubts.

But daylight lends enchantment to the gloomiest of views and some, at least, of Mrs. Brown's worst fears were relieved when Paddington arrived downstairs a little later that morning looking unusually spick-and-span despite his disturbed night.

"I must say you look very smart," she remarked, amid murmurs of approval from the others. "There can't be many bears who sit down to breakfast in evening dress."

"There'll be one less," said Mrs. Bird, striking a warning note, "if certain of them get any marmalade down their front!"

Mrs. Bird had suffered from "bumps in the night" as

well, and with Christmas looming large on the horizon she didn't want her kitchen turned into a bear's ballroom.

Paddington considered the matter for a moment while he tackled his bacon and eggs. He was the sort of bear who believed in getting value for money, and having heard how much Mr. Brown was paying for the hire of his suit, he wanted to make the most of it. All the same, if the Browns were having second thoughts on the subject of dancing, he had to admit that he was having third and even fourth ones himself.

In the past he had often watched dancing programmes on the television and wondered why people made so much fuss, for it all looked terribly easy—just a matter of jumping about the floor in time to some music. But when he'd tried to do it he soon found that even without a partner his legs got tangled up and he shuddered to think what it might be like when he had someone else's in the way as well.

In the end he'd tried doing it on his bed for safety, but that had been worse still—rather like running round in circles on a cotton-wool covered trampolene.

All in all, he decided dancing was much more difficult than it looked at first sight, and to everyone's relief he announced that he was going out that morning in order to consult his friend, Mr. Gruber, on the subject.

Over the years Mr. Gruber had turned up trumps on a variety of subjects and Paddington felt sure he would be able to find something among the many books which lined the walls of his antique shop. Even so, he was still taken by surprise when he arrived at Mr. Gruber's and found his friend doing a kind of jig round his nick-nacks table to the tune from an old gramophone.

Mr. Gruber looked at Paddington sheepishly over the top of his glasses as he drew up a chair. "I have a feeling you won't be the only one with problems tonight, Mr. Brown," he said, panting a little after his exertions. "It's a long time since I last tripped the Light Fantastic."

As Paddington had no idea Mr. Gruber could dance let alone do a Light Fantastic, the news that he was going to Mrs. Smith-Cholmley's ball came like a bolt from the blue, and he grew more and more excited when his friend drew his attention to a large poster in the window.

"Practically anyone who's anyone around here is going tonight, Mr. Brown," he said. "They've got Alf Weidersein's orchestra, and Norman and Hilda Church are bringing their Formation Team."

Paddington looked most impressed as Mr. Gruber went on to explain that Norman Church was a very famous ballroom dancer indeed, and that apart from bringing his team he would be judging the various competitions to be held during the course of the evening.

And when Mr. Gruber, with a twinkle in his eye, reached up to one of the shelves and took down a book on dancing written by Mr. Church himself, Paddington could hardly believe his good fortune. He felt sure if he studied a book written by the man who was actually going to act as judge he ought to do very well indeed.

For the rest of that day, apart from odd strains of the

Veleta and an occasional thump from Paddington's room, number thirty-two Windsor Gardens remained remarkably quiet as everyone got ready for the big event.

Paddington himself was waiting in the hall from quite early on in the evening, clutching Mr. Gruber's book in one paw and an alarm-clock in the other, while he did some last-minute "promenades" by the front door.

Although Norman Church's book was lavishly illustrated with footprints showing the various steps, none of them seemed to go anywhere, and as some were marked "clock-wise" and others "anti-clockwise", he got very confused trying to work out which ones to follow and watch the hands on the clock at the same time.

The book was called LEARNING TO HOLD YOUR OWN ON THE DANCE FLOOR IN TWENTY-FIVE EASY LESSONS, and with only a matter of minutes to go Paddington rather wished Mr. Church had made do with five hard ones instead, for he found it difficult enough getting through the title let alone read the instructions.

All the same, when they set off shortly afterwards he soon joined in the general gaiety, and as they drew near the ballroom he grew more and more excited.

But the journey itself was nothing compared to the atmosphere once they were inside and Paddington peered round with growing interest as he handed his duffle-coat to an attendant.

Strains of music floated out through a pair of double doors at the top of some stairs leading down to the dance-floor, and beyond the stairs he could see couples in evening dress gliding about, their faces lit by twinkling reflections from an enormous mirrored globe revolving high above them.

Mr. Brown cocked an ear to the music as they joined Mr. Gruber and a small queue of other new arrivals. "They're playing 'Goodbye Blues'," he said. "That's one of my favourites."

"'Goodbye Blues'?" repeated Paddington, looking most upset. "But we've only just arrived!"

Mr. Gruber gave a tactful cough. "I think there'll be plenty more tunes before we leave, Mr. Brown."

Bending down, he drew Paddington to one side as the queue moved forward. "I should put your best paw forward," he whispered. "I think you're about to be announced."

Mr. Gruber pointed towards a man in an imposing wig and costume standing at the head of the stairs, and Paddington's eyes nearly popped out as he heard Mr. and Mrs. Browns' names ring out round the ballroom.

"I don't think I've ever been announced before, Mr. Gruber," he replied, hastily stuffing as many of his belongings as possible underneath his jacket.

"Crumbs!" Judy gave a started gasp as she gave Paddington a quick last-minute check. "You've still got your cycle-clips on!"

Catching her daughter's words, Mrs. Brown looked anxiously over her shoulder. "Do take them off, dear," she warned. "You won't feel the benefit otherwise."

Mindful of Mrs. Bird's remarks about keeping his evening-dress clean, Paddington hadn't wanted to take any risks with the trouser bottoms—which tended to slip down rather, and with a forecast of snow in the air he'd decided to make doubly sure. All the same, he did as he was bidden and as he approached the man doing the announcements he bent down.

"Excuse me," he called in a muffled voice. "I'm Mr. Brown and I'm having trouble with my cycle-clips."

"Mr. Cyclops Brown," called the man, in sonorous tones.

"*Cyclops Brown!*" exclaimed Paddington hotly. He stood up clutching his clips, looking most upset that on the very first occasion of being announced his name should have been wrongly called. But by that time the man was already halfway through announcing Mr. Gruber, and Paddington found himself face to face with Mrs. Smith-Cholmley, who was waiting to greet her guests at the foot of the stairs.

"I'm so sorry," said Mrs. Smith-Cholmley, trying to pass the whole thing off with a gay laugh as she took Paddington's paw. "I always thought Cyclops only had one eye . . ." She broke off as she followed Paddington's gaze towards the middle of the dance-floor, for it was all too obvious that Paddington not only had *two* eyes but they were both working extremely well.

"That's Mr. Church," she explained, catching sight of a nattily dressed man posing beneath a spotlight. "He's about to lead off."

As the music started up again Mrs. Smith-Cholmley turned back to Paddington. "Er...I see you've been doing some homework," she continued, catching sight of Mr. Gruber's book in his other paw. "If Mr. Church has trouble with his steps he'll know where to come..." Once again Mrs. Smith-Cholmley broke off, and a look of alarm came over her face. "I didn't say he *has* got trouble," she called. "I only said *if*. It was a joke. I..."

But Paddington was already halfway across the floor. "Don't worry, Mr. Church!" he cried, waving his book. "I'm coming. I think it's all on page forty-five."

Paddington reached the centre of the floor in time to

meet the first wave of advancing dancers. Norman and Hilda Church's Formation Team were just getting into their stride, and if the smile on Mrs. Smith-Cholmley's face had begun to look a trifle fixed, the one Mr. Church presented to his public looked as if it had been indelibly etched for all time.

"Go away," he hissed, as Paddington tapped him on the shoulder. "You're upsetting my Alberts."

Norman Church looked as if he'd just thought up a few more choice items for his chapter on ballroom etiquette, but before he had time to put any of them into words a very strange thing happened.

As his team turned to make a sweeping movement back down the floor a bell started to ring somewhere in their midst.

There was a note of urgency about it which caused the leaders to falter in their stride. In a moment all was confusion as those in the rear cannoned into the ones in front, and in less time than it takes to form up for a Quadrille the damage had been done.

A hard core who thought a fire had broken out behind the bandstand jostled with a group who were equally convinced the floor was about to give way, and they, in turn, ran foul of those who simply wanted to see what was going on.

In the middle of all the hubbub Paddington suddenly reached inside his jacket. "It's all right, Mr. Church," he called, holding up a large, round brass object. "It's only my alarm-clock!"

In the silence that followed Mr. Brown's voice sounded unusually loud. "Two minutes!" he groaned. "That's all the time we've been here. *Two minutes*—and look at it!"

There was no need to suggest looking at the scene on the dance floor, for the rest of the Browns were only too painfully aware of what it was like.

Even Paddington, as he made his way back through the dancers, was forced to admit that he rather wished the floor *had* collapsed, for it would have afforded a quick means of escape from the glances of those around him.

"Never mind," said Judy, going forward to meet him· "We know you meant well."

"Thank you very much," said Paddington gratefully. "But I don't think Mr. Church does."

Casting an anxious glance over his shoulder, he allowed himself to be led off the floor in the direction of some tables to one side of the hall.

"I think I'll sit this one out, thank you very much," he announced, after consulting his book.

Although the chapter on ballroom behaviour didn't include any mention of what to do following the kind of disaster he'd just experienced, there were quite a number of phrases Mr. Church recommended for use when you didn't want to dance and Paddington felt it was a good moment to test one or two of them.

"Not that anyone's likely to ask him after what's just happened," said Mr. Brown, as he whirled past the table a little later on.

"It's a shame really," agreed Mrs. Brown, catching sight of Paddington deep in his book. "He's been practising so hard. I don't like to think of him being a wallflower, and he's been sitting there for ages."

Mr. Brown gave a snort. "Anything less like a wallflower than Paddington would be difficult to imagine," he remarked.

Mr. Brown was about to add pessimistically that the evening wasn't over yet, but at that moment there was a roll of drums and all eyes turned in the direction of the band rostrum as Norman Church climbed up and grasped the microphone in order to announce the start of the competitions.

Now that the dance was in full swing Mr. Church seemed to have recovered his good humour. "Now I want everyone, but everyone to join in," he boomed. "There are lots of prizes to be won...lots of dances...and a special mammoth Christmas hamper for the best couple of the evening . . ."

Mr. Church's words had a livening effect on the ball and during the items which followed he proved his worth as a Master of Ceremonies. He kept up such a steady flow of patter even Paddington began to get quite worked up, and a marmalade sandwich which he'd brought along to pass the time with lay untouched on the table beside him.

It was while the fun was at its height that Mrs. Smith-Cholmley suddenly caught sight of him peering through a gap in the crowd.

"Come along," she called. "You heard what Mr. Church said. Everyone has to join in."

Paddington gave a start. "Thank you very much, Mrs. Smith-Cholmley," he called excitedly. "I'd like to very much."

"Oh!" Mrs. Smith-Cholmley's face dropped. "I didn't mean . . . that is, I . . . er . . ." She looked at Paddington uneasily and then glanced down at her programme. "It *is* the Latin American section next," she said. "I believe you come from that part of the world."

"Darkest Peru," agreed Paddington earnestly.

Mrs. Smith-Cholmley gave a nervous laugh. "I'm not sure if Mr. Weidersein knows any Peruvian dances," she said, "especially dark ones, but we could try our hand at the rhumba if you like."

"Yes, please," said Paddington gratefully. "I don't think I've done one of those before."

Paddington was very keen on anything new, and after slipping the cycle-clips over one of his sleeves for safety, he hastily thrust the marmalade sandwich behind his back, picked up his book, and rose from the table.

"I see you're 'with it'," said Mrs. Smith-Cholmley, mistaking the sudden flurry of movement for a dance step.

Paddington clasped Mrs. Smith-Cholmley firmly with both paws. "I'm never without it," he replied.

Peering round his partner's waist, he consulted the etiquette section of Mr. Church's book again.

"Do you come here often?" he inquired politely.

Mrs. Smith-Cholmley looked down at her feet, both

of which were submerged beneath Paddington's paws. "No," she replied, in a tone of voice which suggested she was rather regretting her present visit. "Haven't you got any pumps?" she asked.

Paddington glanced down at his cycle-clips. "I haven't even got a bike," he exclaimed, looking most surprised.

Mrs. Smith-Cholmley gave him a strange look. "You really ought to have pumps," she said, breathing heavily as she tried to lift her own and Paddington's feet in time to the music. "It would make things so much easier."

Paddington returned her look. He was beginning to get a bit fed up with the way the conversation was going. It wasn't at all like any of the examples in Mr. Church's book, most of which were to do with sitting out on balconies eating snacks. "I think Mr. Brown's got a spare wheel," he replied helpfully. "Have you got a puncture?"

"No," said Mrs. Smith-Cholmley through her teeth, "I haven't. But if you stand on my feet much longer I'm liable to have one!" Paddington's claws were rather sharp and they were digging deeper and deeper into her instep with every passing moment. "I'd be obliged if you would find somewhere else to put your paws."

Paddington relaxed his grasp on Mrs. Smith-Cholmley and tried jumping up and down experimentally a few times. "I don't think I can," he gasped at last. "I have a feeling they're caught in your straps."

To his surprise, when he looked up again Mrs. Smith-Cholmley's face seemed to have gone a very funny colour indeed. And not only that, but she had begun to wriggle

in a way which certainly wasn't included in any of Mr.
Church's illustrations for the rhumba.

"My back!" she shrieked. "My back! There's an
awful creature crawling down my back!" Almost turning
herself inside out, Mrs. Smith-Cholmley reached behind
herself and withdrew something long, golden and glisten-
ing, which she gazed at with increasing horror. "It's all
wet and sticky . . . ugh!"

Paddington peered at the object dangling between
his partner's forefinger and thumb with interest. "I
don't think that's a *creature*, Mrs. Smith-Cholmley," he
exclaimed. "It's a chunk. I must have dropped my
marmalade sandwich down the back of your dress by
mistake!"

Unaware of the drama that was taking place behind

their hostess's back, Mr. Brown gave his wife a nudge. "Good Lord, Mary," he said. "Look at those two. They're going great guns."

Mrs. Brown turned and glanced across the dance floor. "Well I never!" she exclaimed with pleasure. "Who would have thought it?"

But if Mr. and Mrs. Brown were astonished at the sight of the gyrations on the other side of the floor, the rest of the dancers were positively astounded.

One by one the other couples dropped out in order to take a closer look as Paddington and Mrs. Smith-Cholmley, seemingly moving as one, rocked and wriggled in time to the music.

At a signal from Mr. Church, the man in charge of the spotlight concentrated his beam on the two figures, and as Alf Weidersein began urging his orchestra to greater and greater efforts, the shouts of encouragement, the clapping, and the stamping of feet, began to shake the very rafters of the hall.

Paddington himself became more and more confused as he clung to his partner, and far from needing an alarm-clock to show him the way he found himself wishing he'd brought a compass, for he hadn't the least idea where he'd started from let alone where he was going.

From the word go, the winners of the mammoth hamper for the best couple of the evening were never in doubt. Indeed, it would have taken a very brave man indeed to have gone in the face of the cheers which rang out as the music came to an end at last.

For some reason, as soon as willing hands had disentangled Paddington's paws from her shoe straps, Mrs. Smith-Cholmley beat a hasty retreat; and when she did reappear at long last it was in a different dress, but in the excitement this went largely unnoticed.

"A lovely little mover," said Norman Church enthusiastically, turning to Paddington as he presented the prize. "Very fleet. I wouldn't mind using you and your lovely lady in my Formation Team when we do our final demonstration."

Mrs. Smith-Cholmley gave a shudder. "I don't think Mr. Brown and I are open to engagements," she broke in hastily, as she caught a momentary gleam in Paddington's eye.

Paddington nodded his agreement. "I haven't brought any more marmalade sandwiches either, Mr. Church," he said.

"Er . . . yes," Mr. Church looked slightly taken aback. "Talking of marmalade sandwiches," he continued, recovering himself, " what are you going to do with all this food?"

Paddington contemplated the prize for a moment. It was a large hamper. An enormous one, in fact, and it was difficult to picture the many good things there must be inside it.

"I think," he announced, amid general applause, "I'd like to send my half to the Home for Retired Bears in Lima—if it can be got there in time for Christmas. I don't think they can always afford very much extra."

"It'll be done," said Mr. Church. "Even if I have to fly it myself and divide it when I get there."

"There's no need to divide it," said Mrs. Smith-Cholmley, amid renewed applause. "They can have my half as well. After all, there's no time to be lost, and it sounds a very good cause. Especially," she added with a wry smile at her partner, "if the Home's full of bears like Paddington. I wouldn't like to think of them going short of marmalade."

"I wonder what Mrs. Smith-Cholmley meant by that last remark?" said Mr. Brown, as they drove home later that night, tired but happy. He glanced across the front seat. "Have you any idea, Paddington?"

Paddington rubbed the steam from the window with his paw and peered out into the night. "I think it was to do with my chunks, Mr. Brown," he replied vaguely.

Mrs. Brown gave a sigh. Life with a bear was full of unsolved mysteries. "I know one thing," she said. "There may be a lot of deserving cases in the Home—and none more so than Aunt Lucy, I'm sure—but I very much doubt if they have any other bears quite like Paddington."

"Impossible!" agreed Mrs. Bird firmly.

"Absolutely!" said Judy.

"With a capital I," added Jonathan.

But Paddington was oblivious to the conversation going on about him. The first snowflakes of winter were already falling and with the promise of more to come, not to mention the approach of Christmas itself, he was already looking forward to things in store.

"I think," he announced to the world in general, "I shall keep my bicycle clips on in bed tonight. I want to keep myself warm in case I have any more adventures!"